'Gu's unfaltering focus and master̶ persuasive, transformative narrative ̶̶̶̶ ̶̶o had to live like an emotionless machine a̶n̶u̶ eventually comes to acknowledge the very human and universal emotion deep within herself . . . Gu's mastery of storytelling shines'
Kiho Ilbo

'[Gu Byeong-mo] delivers unexpected touches of tenderness within the brutal, exacting world'
The List

'Gu says that the distance between imagination and daydreaming is but a millimetre. She's the writer who beats down the boundary between reality and imagination'
Civic News

'*The Old Woman With the Knife* is a cruel yet beautiful study on what is the fate of being, on bruising and disintegrating life, and on all the inevitable truths of human life'
Chunji Ilbo

'There has never been a Korean novel with such a groundbreaking heroine'
Segye Ilbo

THE OLD
WOMAN
WITH THE
KNIFE

THE OLD
WOMAN
WITH THE
KNIFE

GU BYEONG-MO

TRANSLATED BY CHI-YOUNG KIM

CANONGATE

This paperback edition published in Great Britain in 2023
by Canongate Books

First published in Great Britain in 2022
by Canongate Books Ltd, 14 High Street, Edinburgh EH1 1TE

canongate.co.uk

First published in the United States of America by Hanover Square Press

First published as *Pagwa* in 2013 by Jamobook

1

Copyright © Gu Byeong-mo, 2013
English translation © Chi-Young Kim, 2022

The right of Gu Byeong-mo to be identified as the
author of this work has been asserted by them in accordance
with the Copyright, Designs and Patents Act 1988

British Library Cataloguing-in-Publication Data
A catalogue record for this book is available on
request from the British Library

ISBN 978 1 83885 645 8

Printed and bound in Great Britain by Clays Ltd, Elcograf S.p.A.

MIX
Paper from
responsible sources
FSC® C018072

THE OLD
WOMAN
WITH THE
KNIFE

THE OLD
WOMAN
WITH THE
KNIFE

So this is what it's like on the subway on Friday nights. You feel grateful to discover space just wide enough to slide a sheet of paper between bodies stuck together like mollusks. You're bathed in the stench of meat and garlic and alcohol anytime anyone opens their mouth, but you're relieved because those scents signify the end of your workweek. You momentarily set aside the existential anxiety over whether you would still be taking the subway home at rush hour next year, next month, or even next week. When the doors open at the next station and a river of workers gushes out, she steps in—into their exhaustion, into their visible anguish, into their longing to race home where they can fling their sodden selves onto their beds.

The woman, whose gray hair is covered by an ivory-colored felt hat, is wearing a subdued flower-print shirt, a classic khaki linen coat and black straight-leg pants, and is carrying a brown medium-sized bag on her arm. She is actually sixty-five years old, but the number and depth of the grooves in her face make her look closer to eighty. The way she carries herself and the way she dresses won't leave a strong impression on anyone. The only time anyone pays attention to senior citizens on the subway is when they bump into people as they carry a bundle of discarded newspapers scavenged from one end of the train to the other, or because they're decked out in baggy, purple polka-dot pants, and lugging a pungent bundle of ginger and sesame oil, loudly announcing, "Ouch, my back!" until someone offers them a seat. Sometimes it's for the opposite reason—an older woman forgoing the short, permed style common among the elderly and instead boasting straight white hair to her waist, sun spots inexpertly concealed with powder and eyeliner drawn with a wavering hand, or, even worse, wearing bright red lipstick or a miniskirt suit in pastel colors. The former type of elderly citizen evokes disgust while the latter is so incongruous that onlookers are mortified; regardless, both are one and the same, as people don't want to think about them.

In that sense, she is a model senior citizen, wholesome and refined and respectable. Rather than making a show of how deserving she is of a seat, she stands by the full senior section at the end of the car and doesn't complain. Her clothing is appropriate for a middle-class senior citizen, perfectly aligned with the standard of old age: off-brand but decent clothes, down to her hat and shoes, purchased at Dongdaemun Market or on sale at a department store. Unlike some, she doesn't bellow songs, her face ruddy with drink, taking up space with various kinds of sporting equipment. She exists like an extra in a movie, woven seamlessly into a scene, behaving as if she had always been there, a retiree thrilled to take care of her grandchildren in her golden years, living the rest of her days with a frugality baked into her bones. People stare at their phones, headphones in their ears, shrinking from and swaying with the unending wave of humanity, quickly forgetting that an old person has entered their midst. They excise her from their consciousness as if she's unimportant, recyclable. Or they never even saw her to begin with.

At the next stop, an old man with a cane gets up, hacking up phlegm hard enough to dislodge his internal organs, and she sits down in the vacated seat. She pushes down the brim of her hat and takes a zippered, pocket-sized Bible bound in fake leather out of her bag. An older person opening a Bible on her lap and reading one word at a time, tracing the lines with a loupe, isn't odd or novel in a subway car. Nobody pays any mind as long as she doesn't grab strangers by the arm, ranting about Jesus and heaven and nonbelievers and hell. It's common for the elderly to turn to God late in life, and read Biblical or Buddhist scriptures once death starts bombarding them from all directions—more unusual would be if they were reading *Analects of Confucius* or *Mencius*, a book selection that would reveal intellectual curiosity and an elegance of thought. Even more shocking, especially for an elderly woman, would be to read something by Plato or Hegel or Kant or Spinoza, or *Das Kapital*, which would draw surprised gazes and perhaps doubts as to whether she really understands what she's reading.

With her normal appearance, and behavior that meets societal expectations, she skates under the radar, sitting with her head bowed, reading the enlarged words through her loupe. At some point she raises only her eyes, peering diagonally over her glasses.

She sees a man in his late fifties, standing. He appears to be dozing, holding on to the strap above. His graying hair is tipped in black—perhaps he was too busy to dye his hair again—and he's wearing a leather jacket and black slacks and scuffed black Ferragamo shoes. Looped around his wrist is the sort of clutch bag that is typically stuffed with documents and bills, and carried by debt collectors working for loan sharks. She doesn't take her eyes off him as he sways with the movement of the train.

The man startles awake. Perhaps embarrassed, he suddenly drills his finger into the forehead of a young woman sitting in the seat right in front of him; she looks up, aghast, then looks back to her cell phone, and the man jabs her in the forehead again, a little harder this time. At first, people around them assume she's his daughter, but soon realize they are strangers. "What are you doing, mister?" asks the young woman in a clipped tone, and the man's voice rises, outraged. "Mister? How dare you talk to me like that when you're just sitting there staring at your phone, ignoring the senior citizen in front of you?" People begin murmuring. "I'm pregnant," the young woman says calmly. Hearing that, everyone, including the old woman reading the Bible, casts their eyes reflexively at her belly, but as she's wearing a baby-doll top it's hard to tell if she's showing, though she does look tired and her face is puffy. The man gets louder. "You young girls these days, you don't do your duty. You don't get married or have babies. Instead, you only talk about being pregnant when it's convenient for you. You think I can't tell the difference between pregnancy and being fat from stuffing your face with fried chicken and pigs' feet? And even if you are, are you the only one who's ever been pregnant? Do you think you're the only one to ever have a baby?" He jabs her head after each sentence, not stopping even as the woman swats his finger away a few times. She looks around for help, but all the middle-aged and elderly men sitting around her are avoiding her gaze or faking sleep. She shouts, "Stop picking on me, why don't you pick on these men? I said I'm pregnant!"

The man glances around, and when it seems clear that nobody will come to her aid, he raps her on the head and says, "How dare you lie about being pregnant and talk back to your elder?" The young woman's head smacks into the window behind her and she begins to sniffle, though she is likely not hurt. Finally, a woman in her early fifties, who's sitting across the aisle next to a seat reserved for mothers and pregnant women, gets up and taps the man on the shoulder. "Sir, there's a seat over here." The man grouses and acts as if he's being magnanimous, then sits down, crosses his arms over his bag and closes his eyes.

The older woman approaches the young woman and pats her on the shoulder. "Miss, I mean, mama, don't cry. You can't cry over these things, especially since you'll be a mom soon." She lowers her voice a little. "Don't be upset, not all old people are like him. That man isn't even that old and he just wanted—" Right then there's an announcement that the train will slow in preparation to stop at the next station, and the young woman stands up and screams, "But that's who I had to deal with! So what if not everyone's like him?"

The man in question couldn't have fallen asleep that quickly, but his eyes are closed as if he can't hear the commotion, and the young woman shakes off the other woman's consoling words and steps out onto the platform, although it's unclear whether this is her stop or if she is fleeing the situation. The doors close and the woman in her fifties wavers before sitting down in the now-empty seat, and people around them eye the man disdainfully before letting the incident go. The old woman also drops her gaze back to her Bible. As her work is based on not being noticed, from her behavior to her jewelry, she feels no guilt about her lack of involvement in the altercation.

She wouldn't have involved herself even if nobody had jumped in; she would have placidly observed the young woman's tears and dismay.

Five stops later, with the announcement of the next

station and transfer information, the man opens his eyes and stands up. The old woman closes her Bible and gets up. She stands behind the man, who is now in front of the doors, not too close but close enough that nobody else can slip in between them.

The train stops and the doors snap open like the release valve of a pressure cooker. The platform doors are not quite in line with the train doors. As is often the case at stations where you can transfer to other lines, it's chaotic, with people shoving one another as they get off, and middle-aged women holding bundles are pushing in without waiting, trying to find a free seat. Suddenly, the man stiffens and stops in his tracks, his hand rising to his chest, the clutch bag following suit. He's blocking the way, and people jostle him before he's finally thrust onto the platform.

"Get out of the way!" people call as they try to avoid him, but he continues to block the flow of traffic. A young man rushing toward the transfer point with a large sports bag on his shoulder twists to avoid him, but because the young man is so bulky and tall, the edge of his bag ends up socking the older man in the head. "Oh, sorry," the young man says as he looks back, but the older man is already facedown on the platform, his clutch buried under him. The young man turns pale and looks around frantically as if to broadcast that it wasn't his fault, but people, though they look on with concern, walk by without stopping. Even those who pause stand at a distance so that they won't be roped in to help, their gaze critical of the young man's carelessness and demanding that he take responsibility. At this misfortune the young man is forced to crouch and ask, "Are you okay, sir," shaking him, before he realizes the situation is grave. A public service worker and a station employee rush over to turn the fallen man over, and his frozen, open pupils in his bluish face are like tunnels filled with deep, compacted darkness containing the end of the world. Because they have turned him onto his back, nobody has yet discovered the clean line of the blade that has scored the back of his leather jacket.

In the last bathroom stall she balls up the toilet paper she's unraveled in great quantity, quickly wipes off the remaining poison on the short dagger and flushes the stained paper. She would don surgical gloves at home to meticulously clean the residue. The poison is in the potassium cyanide family and causes paralysis in mere seconds once it enters the bloodstream, so she has to be cautious when she handles it, especially with the recent tremors in her hands. She closes the loupe cover over the dagger; the lens catches the light and twinkles on the metallic walls of the toilet stall. She slides the loupe in her bag before the girls washing their hands at the sink or chatting on the phone detect the flash of light.

She emerges from the bathroom and turns toward the exit, nearly colliding with a group of men. Emergency workers in orange uniforms leap down the stairs and fly over the turnstiles. The force of their movement rustles the front of her coat.

When completing a job in a busy place and turning the corner...

Didn't I tell you not to slow down or stick to the edges but to make a big loop? What if you bump into someone and drop something? You would be announcing, here's all the evidence, to the whole world.

She can recall Ryu's expression when he told her that as if it was just yesterday, and so she will trace the most complicated route home possible. She will exit and walk a block away to a bus stop, and from there she will take the first bus that comes and get off at a subway station on a different line farthest from this place, and go home the long way, tracing the largest orbit on roads spreading out like the fine lines on a palm, staying out as long as she physically can. She strolls leisurely to the exit, toward the glittering darkness overhead.

Around dawn, Hornclaw is wearing gray sweats, about to leave, when Deadweight wakes up. The dog approaches, wagging her tail, and as Hornclaw strokes her head she realizes she neglected to change the drinking water or fill the food bowl last night, exhausted as she was after cleaning up.

"Just wait till you're my age. You keep forgetting things."

The water in the dog bowl has nearly evaporated in the dry air of her apartment, and the few remaining bits of kibble have ossified. Hornclaw tosses the remnants and dunks the bowl in the sink to scrub it. She looks back at Deadweight.

"Although I guess we're about the same age in dog years."

She remembers the vet saying the dog was around twelve years old at their last visit, but she doesn't recall when that was or why she took her in, and those glimmering details mist her mind before vanishing. She can't recall exactly how many years ago she picked her up or where or why—whether the dog looked up at her from a cardboard box on the street with sad, wet eyes. Perhaps, on her way home from a job—though she was used to the repetitive nature of her work, she had still extinguished a life—she was overtaken by an urge that prodded her amygdala with the premonition that if she didn't take this dog home, there would be trouble in the future. What she knows for certain is that she would never have purchased her as a puppy. Even so, she named her Deadweight at the time, feeling foolish for having brought home a living being.

"Want to come with me?" she asks now even though she knows the answer. It's been a long time since Deadweight gave up accompanying her on her morning workouts and stayed behind to nap and laze around.

Hornclaw closes the door and leaves; once she's a block away, she finds herself wondering if she's filled the clean dishes with water and food, and maybe she did fill the food bowl and stuck it in the fridge without thinking, but she's too far from home to turn back now. When she feels that she left the iron plugged in or the stove on or the bath running, she always goes home to check, yet each time she wonders about something like that and hustles home, nothing of the sort actually transpired. Even if she forgot to fill the food bowl it would be fine. It's just dog food, and she's only gone for a few hours of exercise, not days away for a job.

At this point in her life she only goes to the mineral springs in a nearby wooded park. The range of exercise she can do shrinks with every passing year; now only jogging remains as a possibility. Simple exercise equipment like bars or steppers or the elliptical machine, installed for public use by the walking path, only help in maintaining baseline fitness, and she can't remember the last time she used a bench press or a pec-deck machine.

Of course, she can always get a three-month gym membership if she wants to. Her bones and muscles are still strong and it won't be too hard to work those machines. You can see old people sweating and working out in any gym, and near her are two gyms with a few aging machines. But because they're coed, men are always hanging on the machines she needs and she never gets a chance to use them, and on top of that these gyms function less as an exercise space and more as a neighborhood gathering spot. She could go closer to Gangnam and find an exclusive fitness center primarily serving senior citizens in an upscale mixed-use building, but she doesn't want to unless she starts feeling a sense of crisis that she is physically falling apart; in fact, she's already stopped by one of those places and was miffed when the employee at the check-in desk said, "What's your building and unit number?" As if the gym was available only to residents of the complex. The clincher was the employee's surprise when she learned that Hornclaw not only didn't live there but wasn't even from the neighborhood, and asked, "Oh, I see, ma'am, how did you hear about us?" That could have been her way of asking in a warm, friendly way whether Hornclaw had heard of the place by word of mouth or online, but Hornclaw took it to mean *This is not a place for someone like you.* Then the employee went through the various options for maintaining and strengthening aging muscles and told her, "I'm glad you're here as we have a special class that you won't find anywhere else—it's an excellent choice for you." But Hornclaw had already turned away, snapping, "Don't call me ma'am!"

All of this is just an excuse, really, and there's another reason Hornclaw doesn't go to the gym. This is what happens frequently: a male trainer, who isn't even assigned to her, will come up to her as she lies on her back lifting dumbbells and, surprised by her bulging muscles, say, *Ma'am, I can't believe you're over sixty. I've seen few men your age who can do this, let alone women, most of whom think, why bother exercising at this age when the membership fee*—honestly, it's not even that much—*can buy sweets for grandchildren, and anyway what kind of workout have you been doing?* Or other women exercising in the gym will gather around and act too familiar, saying that their mother-in-law who's the same age as Hornclaw refuses to exercise; or invite her to tea, confiding that every week the older folks in the gym get geared up to go hiking together but end up picnicking and drinking and dancing and singing and playing cards. Once, a young woman on the treadmill next to hers held out her business card and said she was a producer for a program that aired at six in the evening and that featured unusual people, and she asked her to come on the show to talk about being an older woman with a killer body. Instead of tearing up her membership card—which still had twenty days left—in front of the producer's eyes, Hornclaw simply chose to stop going to the gym and changed her phone number in order to avoid her trainer's calls.

Once spotted at the gym, younger disease control specialists could probably go on TV and show off their physique and pick up fans or detractors, and smile professionally while freely continuing to do their jobs incognito. Though it's not exactly the same, she knows that the husband of an online retail store CEO, who appeared on cable last year on a show about successful entrepreneurs, was a disease control specialist. Maybe he was just shy—he tried not to be on camera for more than a few seconds at a time, and he didn't look at the camera or smile. But he did end up holding their product and flashing a thumbs-up sign. They made baby food with a mother's care every morning with fresh ingredients, and delivered it. The man, who steamed sweet squash and ground meat and crushed tofu and chopped carrots with the very hands that completed his disease control assignments, brought out feelings of derision and pity in Hornclaw. But as she imagined how his experience with grinding and chopping must have come in handy in this new venture, her thoughts turned magnanimous—it took skill to perform a devoted husband's passivity as he helped his talented wife grow her business, then turn around and become an entirely different person. The key was to create and maintain multiple separate networks that never over-lapped. For Hornclaw, whose use of the internet is limited to sending emails and reading articles, this level of duality would be too difficult and exhausting to execute, and altogether unnecessary for her to master at this late stage in her life.

It couldn't have been because of the broadcast—he was only on screen for less than two minutes total—but Hornclaw heard that the specialist left their line of work at the beginning of the year. Clearly he'd failed to maintain separate spheres. Is he still making baby food with his wife, having accepted that he is now devoted to the family's wholesome business of funneling nutrition and love into their products?

As dawn retreats, the objects around her reveal their forms and the endless comings and goings of the middle-aged and elderly make it harder for Hornclaw to hog the exercise equipment for herself. She leaves the park.

At home, she finds Deadweight's bowls on the floor, properly filled as they should be; the dog must have had breakfast, as the mound of kibble is dented in the middle. Deadweight drops the cloth doll she was gnawing on and jumps up on Hornclaw, and once she feels Hornclaw's hands and the heat of the living she settles back and focuses on her toy again. It's not that she's not fond of her owner; she's learned her human's preferences and understands that she still finds it strange to feel the warmth of a living being and how unbearable it is for her to get used to it. Deadweight is there so that she doesn't lose her way, so that she comes home after work. The dog always maintains an appropriate distance, demonstrating that she is alive in the least intrusive and most optimal way.

At the agency Hornclaw rings the bell on the desk and Worryfixer comes out of the file room, stifling a yawn. Worryfixer knows she's the only one who comes in at this hour, and so they haven't done anything to straighten their rumpled clothes or their unkempt hair.

"What if I'm a client?" Hornclaw demands. "You should be a little more presentable."

"A client would call first. We don't even have a sign."

"Did you sleep in the file room again?"

"I was assisting someone all night. We need to reupholster the sofa in the file room. Maybe with buffalo hide or something? This one's so cheap. The rats have already chewed through it. At this rate I'm going to throw my back out."

"Nobody will stop you if you pay for it." Hornclaw hands over the documents from the completed job. "The Kim case is done. You can write up the report."

"And you confirmed the death, right?" Worryfixer's tone is casual, but Hornclaw is being asked this question more frequently and she's tired of it.

"I know this is part of the process and you're asking as a formality, but if you don't see it in the newspapers why don't you go talk to the reporters on the police beat?"

"I would get nothing. There's another scandal brewing, extensive plans to cover up corruption among National Assembly members."

"I wouldn't know about that, they do that all the time. I'm just offended that you don't trust this old lady."

"Oh, I know how thorough you are. I've been around for ten years! But…"

"But?"

"Mr. Sohn wants us to follow procedure these days, so."

Hornclaw understands. Worryfixer smooths it over quickly but Hornclaw can feel Sohn's suspicions. Her sixty-fifth birthday passed a while ago, and regardless of what industry she's in she's at an age where even a desk jockey tasked with mundane, trivial work might be pressured to retire. Of course Sohn would be nervous. In this line of work, if adaptability, judgment and physicality aren't in perfect harmony, it's a serious problem, one that threatens not only the agency's work but also the disease control specialist's own life. She can imagine Sohn's expression as he just waits for her to get clumsy or make a tiny mistake, and become more harm than good for the agency.

This isn't a situation where she can pull rank and say, *Sohn, I was already doing this work when your own father was the very young head of this agency. I practically changed your diapers.* If that worked, the agency would be no different from the many small, poorly run family businesses out there that fail to fire musty, old, useless employees because of history and nostalgia. Moreover, it would be insulting to be treated like a sack of old bones moldering in the back room. She always believed she would step away if Sohn ever hinted that he wanted to get rid of her, but for now they still call her Godmother out of respect for her status as an original partner.

She's taken a monthly salary all this time because it's inconvenient to have to manage the money herself, but the actual sum she's earned and entrusted with the agency—supposing they haven't squandered it all at this point—should be sizable. If she wants to retire, all she has to do is cash in her stake. Considering where the market is right now, it probably won't be enough to purchase a building she could rent out, but she could set up a small fried-chicken-and-beer joint in a residential area, and as long as she doesn't expand the business too fast or become the victim of gentrification or get swindled and lose everything, she might be able to live the rest of her life in peace. She doesn't have greedy offspring who would meddle and drain the coffers, or any family at all to look after, so it would be plenty for her and Deadweight. Even though she isn't one to listen encouragingly to strangers' stories or make friends or joke with guests or soothe drunks, she should end up fine; being a cruise director isn't a requirement to succeed in a simple business like that.

No matter what your occupation is, once you're in your fifties you could be managing staff one day, then forced to retire the next. She's often seen executives use their retirement packages to set up a restaurant near their former employers, and these executives are lauded for embarking on a new chapter in their lives. But these days, with the recession, you're lucky if, after having found yourself in your youth—and even if you didn't actually find yourself, or even come to realize that you never had a self to begin with—

you can prepare for your old age by opening a store or holding on to real estate. It's hard enough to live without incident through your twenties and thirties and forties, let alone old age. Since Hornclaw can cash in her assets anytime she wants to, hers would be a much more elegant retirement than most. No tiptoeing around one's children for pocket money or, even more pitifully, rotting irrelevantly away in a one-room rental somewhere.

Despite the many possible roads she could have taken to relax and sink into an armchair, she had insisted on hands-on disease control work all this time. It wasn't just because she would feel anxious and empty if she stepped away. There aren't that many retired disease control specialists who enjoy a good final act, as "retirement" for a longtime operative tends to mean a violent death in the field, but there are a select few who have gone into the restaurant or dry cleaning business or even retreated into Buddhist temples. What gets in the way of safe retirement is the unique nature of disease control. It isn't quite like having an obsessive habit or an addiction, but it is, in some ways, similar to being addicted to drugs or gambling in that it's difficult to extricate yourself from it. Trying to picture someone who has been killing people for forty-five years frying chicken or dry-cleaning clothes is like trying to imagine an old wolf incubating an egg. But Hornclaw believes that if you didn't die on the job, you should erase as much of your past as possible and enjoy a restful, leisurely retirement.

She sometimes wonders what difference it makes to take away ten or forty-five years from a life, when the essence of life is continuous loss and abrasion that leaves behind only traces of what used to be, like streaks of chalk on a chalkboard. She never presumed she herself would live out her natural life and so she wouldn't mind leaving this world through an untimely death. Each time she approaches Sohn, confident that she's ready to retire, somehow she can't bring herself to do it.

It's not an appealing line of work. I won't say I do it because someone has to. It's laughable to say it's for justice. But if the money I make by getting rid of vermin can be used later, that doesn't seem to be a bad thing, does it?

At one time, she imagined sharing meals and ordinary moments like walking in the snow with the man who told her that. Everyday scenes she wasn't supposed to wish for, days she couldn't have, because he might have sneered at her.

"Hello." Bullfight enters through the back door, prying Hornclaw from her thoughts. "Oh, look, it's Granny."

Even before the door swung open, the unpleasant scent of fougère announced his appearance. Nothing good would come from seeing him. Hornclaw signs the document Worryfixer holds out and accepts the thick envelope that contains information about her next job. She shoves it in her bag as she turns away.

Bullfight grabs her by the arm. "Where are you going, Granny? Stay a little. It's been a while." He scratches his unruly mass of hair.

This kid is in his early- to midthirties, a little younger than Worryfixer, and though he is always rude to her, he's valued greatly by Sohn for his client relations. At first, Hornclaw thought the kid was out of his skull for wearing cologne, but she was told that this was in fact his natural scent and that he uses deodorant to neutralize it when he goes out to a job—a lot of hogwash, truly, since she's fully aware how young, talented disease control specialists like to make their mark, like a dog pissing on utility poles.

Like his stupid alias, the way he speaks is immature and lazy and his attitude disrespectful and unfocused, and he dresses like an alcoholic who's lost his business and his house and everything in it, from the wardrobe to the dining table, and is a step away from having to sell his kidney. In fact, he is the exact opposite of a drunk, with a surprisingly confident expression, a disdain for alcohol and cigarettes because they slow him down, and a closet full of expensive suits he wears for dealing with important people. It goes without saying that he has the attributes required of a disease control specialist—speed, accuracy, precision—and on top of that he also has a talent for customer service. While some in the industry care only about the outcome, Bullfight indulges his clients' most ridiculous requests. In standard cases, all you need is two days at most to find and eliminate the target, especially if the target is in the country, but some clients want to invoke fear in their targets first, forcing them to marinate in anxiety before being dispatched in the most gruesome way possible. And then there are requests that are truly cumbersome and deranged, like asking that the target's fingers be chopped off joint by joint and sent to the client, or that their arms and legs get broken first. In those cases Bullfight would stage the necessary scene, put it all together and circle the target for as long as three months before doing the actual deed.

As the strange occurrences and suspicions multiply, the target becomes so troubled that he can barely breathe; the target finally sees how his life has been ruined, and right before he loses his mind, Bullfight shows his true colors. At this stage, a disease control specialist must be in tune with the target's psyche so precisely that he doesn't have a chance to go completely insane: Bullfight turns the screws before backing off, because killing someone who has gone crazy becomes an act of mercy, which goes against the client's desires. He then slowly begins the final stage of the process in the cruelest way, within the limits allowed by the situation, though more often he changes the circumstances for his own convenience. According to Sohn, even though the kid seems to enjoy himself, he never smiles or shows excitement; rather he is a calm and steady surgeon, a consultant meeting with a customer.

Of all the many strange requests that come in, Bullfight refuses just one thing: a video of the disease control process or scene. Of course, from the agency's perspective the rule is to never hand over to the client what might end up as evidence, but for Bullfight it's not to protect trade secrets or to shield the client from seeing something brutal. It's because he bristles at the demand, considering the request an insult to his professionalism and lack of trust in his work.

If Hornclaw had to point to unexpected aspects of the kid's personality, it would be his special forces background—though there was no way, or need, really, to confirm if it was true—and the way he gathers more research than necessary, beyond what the agency provides, even if he trashes it all later. Also unusual are his prolific reading of books, though who knows where or how he is using that trait, and, above all else, his preference of showing up in person at the agency to accept his assignments, like Hornclaw does. Though she goes in sporadically because that is how she has always done it throughout her long career, most young specialists are given assignments and associated research online.

Though she's heard Sohn's praises and Worryfixer's stories over the last three years, Hornclaw has probably laid eyes on Bullfight at most four times, and each time he smirked and needled her.

Even during their very first encounter.

"With your stature, Granny, don't you have to be a little more skilled than people who walk in off the street?" he asked when first introduced to Hornclaw. "When I saw you, you didn't look much different from a housewife stabbing a brisket with a kitchen knife."

At first, Hornclaw thought she would be generous, since the kid was young enough to be her son. "Only if you're trying to look cool. I'm glad that I look like a housewife. The result is what's important, not whether you're using a kitchen knife or a filleting knife. Anyway, how would you know how I use a knife?"

"You did that Park case, remember? I was watching you, Granny. When you stabbed, it went straight in, but you keep turning your wrist out when you slash. Do you do that on purpose? Or is it just a bad habit? I guess it might depend on the kind of knife you're using, but you should know that you can't cause a fatal injury that way. You can't even expect severe bleeding."

Hornclaw was stunned that she hadn't detected someone approaching the scene—the kid's talent for creeping was certainly more advanced than the acuity of her senses—but at the same time she wanted to praise the kid for noticing her longstanding habit in a situation that couldn't have lasted more than three minutes.

She paused for a moment. "I thought I sensed someone watching. I figured I'd get rid of him, too. But that was you, I see. It might have been a little less convenient because I twisted that way, but I didn't miss my mark. I can't tell you where you can and can't be, but don't come to someone else's work site and snoop."

Bullfight's lip curled.

She knew he was thinking, *I know you didn't know I was there.*

"Why, because it's distracting? You think you could catch me if you came after me, Granny?"

Bullfight's expression reminded Hornclaw of a baby kicking and cooing, and she felt herself smile faintly. "Who knows? But it's basic courtesy not to distract a colleague when she's working. Put yourself in my shoes."

"Oh, so you get distracted, Granny? Not me. Even if you come right up to my face and stare at me, I can keep doing what I was doing. Isn't it a given that you need to be able to concentrate in this line of work?"

Realizing that this little punk was making fun of an old woman's surely diminished senses and mental strength, Hornclaw decided that he wasn't cute anymore. "Go play somewhere else. I'm too old for this."

She was about to leave when Bullfight asked suddenly, "Granny, you have kids?"

Hornclaw paused before ignoring him and turned on poor Worryfixer. "Tell Sohn that he needs to get a grip on his favorite employee. Why is this fetus taking the census all of a sudden?"

"I'll take care of it," Worryfixer said, looking sternly down at Bullfight as he scraped at a hangnail with a large butcher knife.

Hornclaw was annoyed by her own laxity; not only had she gotten mired in a conversation with a stupid kid, but she had also nearly softened toward him. "It's not just that. It's basic courtesy for colleagues to keep their distance. Have things changed that much? Do the others hang out and grab dinner after work? Am I being too old-fashioned here?"

Worryfixer waved their hands. "No, no, Godmother. Of course not. You're right. I'll give you a call next..."

Hornclaw turned and left without letting Worryfixer finish, closing the door behind her. That was two months ago.

Now, Hornclaw tries to hide her surprise.

Bullfight seems to have detected her agitation. "It's getting colder in the mornings. If you go around that early without any hot packs, your knees are going to ache."

The reason she's disturbed is because she immediately attempted to yank her arm out of his grip but failed; now she's jittery, feeling her physical decline in spite of her best efforts. A plant beyond harvest is bound to be scraggly, and a young man is obviously stronger than an older woman, but she's a specialist just like him.

Bullfight slowly relaxes his grip on her arm, but Hornclaw sinks down into the sofa, disappointed by her physical weakness.

"Have you thought about growing your nails?" Bullfight asks.

She looks at him, wondering what lunacy this is. The kid draws his finger down the bulging blue vein on the back of her hand; his fingernail feels like a metal implement scratching her. The thin skin of her hand, layered with deep wrinkles, looks like it could give off years of accumulated dust, and if you follow the veins to her round nails, which have a dull peachy hue and are trimmed neatly to one millimeter in length as usual, it's easy to see three of them are smashed in, likely to turn black soon, judging from their color.

"Because it's such a waste," Bullfight continues. "And pathetic. You used to be known as Nails, and even if you're not as sharp as you used to be, at least you could grow out your real nails and paint them in a rainbow of colors."

She yanks her hand away, not even wanting to retort, *If I grew them out I would slash your face so that you couldn't even begin to attempt to jigsaw it back together,* and Bullfight smiles as if he's accomplished what he's been after.

"Don't you have someone to show yourself off to, if you were to doll yourself up like that?" Bullfight leers.

What the hell? Her heart stops, but her expression

doesn't change. Then again, she might believe she's maintaining a calm, unruffled exterior, but he could have caught the corner of her upturned mouth or one eye trembling ever so slightly. She suppresses the urge to blurt, *How do you know that*—which would amount to digging her own grave—and actually it would be better to retort, *What is this nonsense, what evidence do you have*, and grab him by the throat—as she fingers the Buck knife in the inner pocket of her jacket. She tries to discern if he detects her injury, the one sustained a month ago but she never told anyone about. The kid's expression is untroubled and bright.

Show yourself off? To whom? Worryfixer has no idea what Bullfight is referring to. The two disease control specialists exchange glances, a smirking curiosity from Bullfight and a tense wariness from Godmother, nothing more. Though Worryfixer is intrigued by this conflict, it's a problem for later. They've caught on that Godmother's trying her best to conceal her hostility and murderous rage, and they understand that this granny is prepared to kill the industry's rookie and MVP.

Hornclaw calms herself and takes her hand off the Buck knife. "I don't know what you mean."

She gets up, ignoring the pain that visits her from time to time, the pain that stabs her in the lower back.

She started to creak over a decade ago, but ever since she got in trouble on that job a month back, she has been feeling seriously bad, the pain constantly flexing and sending jolts.

Worryfixer pushes Bullfight into the file room with both hands. "Godmother hasn't done anything to you, so stop bothering her. Go on, I have that file you asked for."

For her part, Hornclaw understands what Worryfixer is concerned about. Violence among fellow operatives is common, but it has long been forbidden to murder someone due to a personal grudge, and in order to maintain that rule, the agency only takes one job if it gets inquiries from two clients whose interests might be at odds with one another. If the rejected client goes to another agency, fine—it's more important to foster an atmosphere of trust than it is to chase a fee—and if a specialist violates this unspoken rule and kills for his own personal agenda, the other operatives track down the violator and make sure it doesn't happen again. They do this by removing a body part necessary for this line of work; usually it's a hand or a foot or, sometimes, an eye. So when Hornclaw was fingering her knife, it wasn't to let out the rage trapped in her body and cut his throat; it was more of a habit or a prayer.

★ ★ ★

You can't last in this line of work if you show your feelings. It doesn't matter if it's rage or discomfort or regret. The most important thing is to let insults wash over you. And you're a woman, which means you'll often have to ignore insults.

Ryu had flung a glass ashtray at her head after saying these words. She wasn't ready. She ducked instinctively, but it grazed her hair, hit the wall behind her and exploded into shards, scratching her.

You shouldn't have ducked. Good reflexes are beside the point. The most important skill is being able to read the situation. What if it was your target who got so angry that he threw the ashtray at you? If you duck like that, he would have to be an idiot not to get suspicious about who you really are. Of course, the worst would be if you automatically catch whatever is thrown at you.

Nails, of all things. The kid, jeering like that, looking down on her longstanding nickname, clearly wants to get under her skin; Hornclaw doesn't understand why the fetus is pestering her. What does he want with an old woman? This can't be that entertaining for him. Did Sohn give him a secret assignment to poke her until she quits? That can't be an effective strategy, since they don't bump into each other that often.

It wasn't just that she was known as Nails when

she was young; she had been known by that name for a long time, until well into her midforties, and it was also an easier name to remember than her alias, Hornclaw, which was given to her by the first head of the agency, the man who was in charge even before Sohn's father. The name signified aggression, but an animal's horns and claws were protective as well. She never thought the alias suited her. Nor her nickname, as she had never once grown her nails long or painted them, but the head of the agency at the time was impressed by her sharp, exacting skills and her way of finishing neatly. Soon, every time she was sent to a client, the boss would joke, "I'll send the one with the long nails," even though she was the only specialist available, and it stuck.

Clipping one's nails short and leaving them bare is one of the hundreds of passive ways to conceal one's strength. Short, smooth nails that look like they can't even mark rubber clay conceal the aggression inherent in the owner of the fingernails.

Hornclaw passes by clothing shops and beauty stores packed in the underground shopping area by the subway station and finds herself stopping in front of a nail shop. The manicurists, with their hair dyed yellow or red, sit in straight lines, holding and looking down at the customers' hands as if praying, and the young female customers leave both hands on the table in front of them, patiently maintaining the same position, though sometimes they stretch or twist. All of that brings to mind Arab thieves right before their hands are chopped off as punishment.

Hornclaw was already past fifty by the time nail art became popular and salons popped up everywhere, and, puzzled by these women who entrusted their hands to someone else, as if in handcuffs, she had walked blithely by. Later, after she discovered what went on in those places and she happened to have time to waste since work had dried up a bit, she grew somewhat curious, but figured she was too old—who was she trying to impress at her age with that frivolous nonsense? And anyway it would be inconvenient to get the polish removed once she got an assignment. At the time, she didn't know that artificial nails were glued on and believed she would have to grow out her own.

Someone to show herself off to.

Vague images sharpen as she recalls Bullfight's voice. She didn't know that still existed inside her— the traces of desire she thought had vanished long ago and remained missing. She furrows her brow. Nails? She was accustomed to closing the door on that kind of desire before it bloomed and seeped out of her pores. But now, her eyes are drawn to things without function, things that exist just to be pretty.

All because of what that kid said to her, his voice muddy with mockery and malice.

She draws closer and studies the artificial nails displayed in the window. Delicate flower petals that look as if they would tremble and fall off the edge of a heartbroken girl's hands, a lavender bird so vivid that it seems like it could fly away, a colorful, abstract design. Everything is pretty, but she can't see each and every detail because she is farsighted, and the many colors and patterns resemble the lacerations and scars hidden all over her body.

The manager spots the older woman who keeps inching backward and squinting at the display, and, still holding the hand of a girl in a school uniform, she calls out, "Ma'am, would you like to get your nails trimmed? Please take a seat, I'll just be a moment."

The schoolgirl looks at Hornclaw, then frowns and scoots sideways, as if she's worried that the stench of old age might rub off on her. Hornclaw encounters that reflex eighty to ninety percent of the time when she sits down on the subway, and it's inconvenient to feel offended by it each and every time. Anyway, Hornclaw is hesitating for an unrelated reason.

The manager mentioned trimming because the old woman's attire and appearance are frugal and simple, and she thinks this old lady wouldn't want new nails with sparkles and patterns and beads on them. Of course, no matter who the customer is, she would diligently massage hand cream into each nail and wrap her hands in a hot towel. The manager is unaware that Hornclaw is hesitating because her nails are already clipped short with nothing left to trim, and, more importantly, because she is not ma'am. Hornclaw falters, then heads quickly toward the subway entrance, and feels rather than sees the artificial nails on the other side of the window dancing dizzily as if they are released and chasing her.

It's a regular checkup, not one that employs cutting-edge equipment to power wash every cell in her body. At the health clinic, the cursory checkups for those over forty include a basic blood test and an exam that is mostly a formality, along with chest X-rays and blood pressure measurements; these screenings don't ferret out problems more serious than a heightened risk for diabetes. Costs rise steeply when you start imaging other parts of your body and drawing blood for multiple screenings, and, more critically, it's a bother to undergo complicated steps and procedures, like having to fast or drinking CT contrast. The most inconvenient one is the endoscopy. Other than the sedation, the government covers most of the procedure. It would be unpleasant to swallow the endoscope without being put under, but it's also impossible to imagine she would be comfortable lying unconscious in front of someone else, defenseless.

Still, Hornclaw never forgoes her annual checkup. If she were to skip even that, fail to confirm that her blood pressure is just barely in the normal range and that she doesn't have diabetes, it would be akin to giving up on herself. The moment you accept your changing, sagging body, you'll fail at your next job or, if you're lucky, the one after that, and failure in this line of work often results in the disease control specialist's death.

Before she can give her name at the front desk Nurse Park recognizes her and bows in greeting. Hornclaw crosses the hallway, lined with exhausted parents who look as if they won't care if the world ends two days from now and kids crying from fever or stomachache. While she came today in an effort to avoid the weekend rush, there are still so many patients; it's cold season. She checks the clear acrylic sign on the door of Room 3 for the name of the doctor on duty and settles in to wait.

This general clinic in a crumbling building is open every single day, from nine in the morning until eleven at night, and is limited to internal medicine, orthopedics, ENT and pediatrics, staffed by contract doctors taking shifts. The neighborhood residents come here late at night with simple ailments, like a fever or a child's stomachache, instead of heading to an emergency room at a university hospital. Because the doctors aren't on a regular schedule, there's no guarantee that someone you saw two days ago will be the one you see today. The clinic doesn't have those new cash cow imaging machines, so doctors refer patients with serious symptoms to large hospitals. These days, as medicine continues to be privatized, the clinic is becoming less relevant beyond a place to come to in the middle of the night. Even five years ago, Hornclaw remembers, there wasn't an empty seat in which to wait. She's now quickly summoned into the exam room.

After listening to her heart, Dr. Chang puts his stethoscope down and nods at young Nurse Kim, who is standing next to him. Nurse Kim hesitates for a moment, not quite used to this situation yet, before leaving and closing the door behind her. She is still new, having started working here about six months ago, and at first when Dr. Chang signaled for her to leave them in private, which he did every time the old woman made a visit, she looked at the two of them in a puzzled manner. By this point, even though she's still confused, she leaves without a word, hav-

ing learned like all newbie nurses to refrain from asking questions when a doctor requests something. Of
course, the nurses whisper among themselves, making up scenarios—much of it involves soap opera level
speculation about the old woman who comes in every
other month, asking only for Dr. Chang regardless
of her symptoms. The old lady leaves without a prescription most of the time so why does she bother
coming in, they wonder, and every time he exam-
ines her Dr. Chang sends out the nurse after listening
to the old lady's heart, which clearly means the two
are having a thrilling extramarital affair in their old
age. Even though it couldn't be an affair, as one person has never married and the other is a fifty-eight-
year-old divorcé, they like to exaggerate. Perhaps it's
because their relationship can't be explained within a
traditional context.

"If you've been experiencing any symptoms, you
have to tell me," Dr. Chang says. "I'd still have to
know even if we don't include it in your file."

"My lower back is hurting, but it's not too bad."

"Should I give you a referral to orthopedics?"

"I don't want any record of this."

"I can tell them in person. I can tell them it would
be good for you to get some physical therapy."

"All I need is a pain-relief patch."

"All right, then."

"That must not be all you want to say to me today," Hornclaw says.

"It's not? What do you mean?" Dr. Chang studies her records on the computer monitor to see if he forgot something.

Hornclaw is taken aback. Is it possible he doesn't know?

"You don't seem to have any major issues. The last time you came with any symptom at all—it was a fever and a cold—was six months ago. If you're worried about anything else, like bone density or something hard for us to measure here, I'll write you a referral. If you're worried about your memory, like if you find your phone in the fridge or your wristwatch explodes in the microwave, well, that's unfortunately nature's course, so I don't really have much to say about that. It's a little odd for me to tell you this when I'm seven years younger, but I can tell I'm not the way I used to be, even though I take care of myself. But I don't think you'll develop dementia as long as you keep working. Of course, your predisposition for the disease doesn't only depend on your daily habits, so you can get tested if you're nervous. I think, in your case, it'll be a waste of time."

Hornclaw is indeed curious to know what is within

the realm of normal, including how steeply her memory will diminish as she ages. But that isn't what she's expecting to hear from Dr. Chang today. If he knows what's happened but has decided not to meddle and is now pretending to be completely in the dark—well, Dr. Chang has a superb poker face. Then again, he would have to be this circumspect, since he has maintained a close relationship with the agency for nearly fifteen years. He is a gruff but hardworking neighborhood doctor who treats the disease control specialists and their large and small injuries and illnesses and sells them all kinds of drugs. This cooperative relationship is only possible because Dr. Chang is the proprietor of the clinic.

"Oh…well, so… That's not what I mean."

"Are you concerned about something else?"

It does seem that Dr. Chang doesn't know anything about that night a month ago, the night she made a fatal error that nearly ended her life, an error that mocked her idle daydreams of running her own fried chicken place.

"No. Thank you." Hornclaw gets up. Dr. Chang must really not know about that night or he's pretending not to. Either way, she's grateful.

"Should I send the results to the agency, as always? Or to you directly?" Dr. Chang asks delicately, in con-

sideration of their growing old together. He's specifically asking if he should send the results to her home
should they be bad, if he should tip her off before the
agency so she can prepare for retirement on her own
terms, but Hornclaw smiles and shakes her head.

"It's fine. You can send it to Worryfixer."

"Still confident, I see!"

It isn't confidence. Hornclaw doesn't want to be
pitied by the agency. If she was asked when exactly
she would accept that she is no longer of use, precisely
on which birthday, what would she say?

She doesn't want to think about that right now.
She's come this far somehow because she's managed
not to die; it wasn't as if she was ever in a position to
dream about her future or plan for retirement. She's
still all right. Her heart thumps reliably, and though
her muscles spasm sometimes and she's out of breath
at others, she has never felt disoriented, wondering
where she was, what she was doing or why she was
doing it. The parts that comprise who she is haven't
deteriorated yet.

Still, she doesn't feel fully relieved as she leaves the
clinic. If Dr. Chang really is in the dark about what
happened that night, then her accidental coconspirator
has stayed silent. Why? No matter how strong their
promise was, no matter how iron willed a person he

was, the events of that day had been so unusual she was unsettled by his behavior.

That night a month ago, Hornclaw finished a job near a reservoir in K County with a rare bout of hand-to-hand combat, caused by the impressive resistance of her agile target and, more problematically, her own carelessness.

The target was a man in his fifties who peddled taxi licenses illegally, and as if to prove that he had lived a long life filled with shady acts, he quickly caught on that he was being tailed and began driving fast, swerving this way and that. Even though Hornclaw knew she'd been discovered, she followed him as he sped away.

On a narrow, deserted two-lane road so dark that she had to turn on her high beams, Hornclaw roared up to his car and pulled up perpendicular to make him stop; the target, who had been speeding along at 90, reflexively braked and jerked the wheel, careening off the edge of the road and down the slope. She confirmed through her rearview mirror that the car was tumbling down and attempted to reduce her speed, but she was already going so fast that she triggered the automatic brakes and her head smashed into the steering wheel.

Feeling dazed, she got out and saw the target's arm poking out from under his car, which had flipped over like a turtle and kicked up dust, and if she were younger she would have remembered to first cut the tendons of the hands and feet to check if the target was still conscious, which would have destroyed any remaining fighting spirit. This time, in the hazy, hot darkness, she made a grave error and decided she would pull the target completely out of the wreckage before killing him. Alas, the target had been pretending to be unconscious, and as soon as he emerged he snatched both of her ankles and pulled, causing her to fall back onto a sharp rock too quickly for her to execute a safe fall. Before she could get up, the target's heavy body slammed into hers.

She was so small that in all of her years in this line of work she had never fought anyone smaller and lighter than her, but it was the first time in a long while that she had found herself fighting with such a tall man; was that the reason for the tightness in her chest? Her heart was pounding and she was starting to lose her breath, and the target succeeded in yanking her hat off. When he confirmed that she was a woman, he suddenly grew confident, springing up triumphantly and kicking her repeatedly in her ribs, rolling her down the steep slope.

"You made a big mistake," he said, grunting. "You think you can get me? Who sent you? Shit, and you're a grandma! Even if you were young and pretty I might not have let you go. Who sent you? You want to live? Then go tell them. Next time, send a better bitch. Okay? If there aren't enough girls, at least send a guy my size. What the hell is this?"

Every time his voice went up at the end of a question, he kicked harder, as if staying on the beat, and Hornclaw tumbled all the way to the bottom of the slope and gripped a thatch of tangled weeds in an effort not to be shoved into the reservoir.

"Talk! Who sent you?"

Grimacing, Hornclaw let out a sneer. In her forty-five years of disease control, she had almost never known who had sent her.

The target grabbed her by the scruff of her neck and mashed her head into the ground, cranking her arm behind her back. "You're laughing? Are you seriously laughing right now?" He leaned his weight on her back. "Who are you?" His breath was hot against her ear.

The fact that he didn't instantly know who was behind this and was pestering the hired assassin showed that he suspected more than a few people, highlighting the kind of life he had been living, Hornclaw thought derisively, and, her knees bent and her head still shoved in the mud, she murmured, "How old are you, anyway?"

Of course she knew from his file that he was fifty-three, and she even remembered all sorts of trivial information about him, like when, where and how many times he met up with his current mistress.

"How can such a young piece of shit be so rude to an elder on our first meeting?" she said, her voice low.

That was when the target flinched, let go of her wrist and looked down. A knife stuck deep in his chest shivered in the night air. He instinctively brought his shaking hands to the knife, but he fell over before he could touch the handle. Hornclaw got to her feet. All the blood in his body would have rushed toward the blade piercing his heart, draining his limbs of strength; even his breath was stuck in his throat. The target's head was now by her feet, and his eyes darted and glistened; if she kicked him in the forehead, they might pop out of their sockets and roll along the ground.

She kicked his body to move him onto his back. Perhaps knowing what she was about to do next, the target's hands reached toward her, as if to hang on to her legs.

With her foot she batted his hands away and stomped on the handle of the knife, as if making sure a half-smashed writhing worm was really dead, and through the soles of her shoe she felt the reverberation as the thick muscles and veins in his heart were severed. Pushing the handle of the knife back and then forward with her toe, she looked down placidly as the target's hands and feet shuddered and fell limp.

"You're not that smart, are you? I figured as much. If you're going to overpower someone, you have to search them first to see if they have any weapons. I gave you so much time, but you were so excited that you couldn't get it together," Hornclaw muttered, even though she knew the target couldn't hear anything anymore.

And anyway, she didn't say it because she thought he would hear her, but rather because she thought Ryu would say something like that if he were next to her; it had become a habit of hers to embody Ryu and talk to herself, as if casting a spell.

Hornclaw stuffed the body in a sack and loaded it into her trunk. Then she put on thick disposable plastic booties with elastics around the ankles, used for disinfection and sterilization, and went back down the path she had tussled with the target, smudging out the prints with her feet, taking care to make it look as natural as possible. One problem was the flipped-over car; since she couldn't pick it up and move it, she left the indentation where she'd dragged the target out of the driver's seat. Using the shoes she took off his feet before she returned to the scene, she stamped footprints going up the slope. It was an approximation, but she maintained about two feet between each print, the average adult male's stride, and she kept pushing and gliding her own bootie-clad feet to remove her traces. The story would be that a man accidentally flipped his car over, crawled out on his own, went up to the road to ask for help, then went mysteriously missing. It wouldn't be an entirely bad thing for the police to become suspicious of the tracks and go fish around in the reservoir; no matter whose body came out, it wouldn't be the target's, and she could buy some time while that happened. There were no CCTVs on that remote stretch of road. Since the cars themselves hadn't crashed into each other there wouldn't be metal or glass bits scattered across the road, and even if there were they would be meaningless pieces that could have come from any number of cars. Though she was concerned about the visible skid marks it would be difficult to immediately determine whose they were, and days would pass while they were figuring it out as other cars drove over them.

She rubbed her dim eyes while she looked around

with her flashlight, collecting everything she could find, down to a single strand of hair. She initially thought it was just her aging eyes, but she began to feel immensely drowsy, everything lurching around her, and she realized that it might be connected to the back injury she'd suffered when she landed on the rock earlier. The blood began to pool in her clothes, and realizing the potential evidence, she found the rock in question and dug it out of the ground. She looked around carefully for any scraps of fabric left behind.

She loaded the rock and trash and other little bits of evidence she'd collected next to the body and took one last look around before turning on the ignition. It might have been better if the target's car had been driven into the water so that evidence of the accident could have gone undiscovered until the next time the reservoir was drained. No matter what she did she wouldn't be able to move the destroyed vehicle, and there were other problems, like oil stains, that she couldn't deal with in her injured state.

It was already four in the morning by the time she sped to the memorial park at S City, and though it was outside regular crematorium hours, Choi, the care-taker whom she'd contacted on the way, was waiting at the entrance to the parking lot. He immediately popped open her trunk and hauled the sack over his shoulder, and Hornclaw followed silently.

Choi walked into the crematorium, put the body on a tray, opened the door to the nineteenth slot at the very end without delay and turned on the switch. "Do you have anything else to put in?"

Hornclaw fumbled with the target's shoes and put them on the tray.

"Really? You know it's not so easy to incinerate leather," Choi grumbled.

"Just fire it for longer, then. This isn't your first time doing this."

Choi waved his hand, signifying perhaps both his irritation and assent, but when she took the heavy rock from the sack and put that on the tray, he looked like he was on the verge of cursing at her. "Come on. You know a rock won't burn at all. Do I really need to say that out loud?"

"Just fire it as much as you can and leave it out somewhere in the park. There are rocks everywhere." Knowing that Choi would get all the work done quickly and accurately despite the grousing, she turned away after the tray went in. "You can send the bill to Worryfixer, as always."

"Leather shoes and a rock… This time I'm going to charge double, I'm telling you."

She thought she could feel on the back of her neck the heat from the flames enveloping the target and the other random artifacts, which was probably due to the pain radiating out from her wound.

She hadn't had the chance to check if she was still bleeding, but something hot kept trickling down her back and her vision grew hazier as her eyes drooped. Blood soaked through the back of her pants but she had to keep driving. If she pulled over for a quick break, she might not be able to open her eyes again. She braced against the wheel with one hand and attempted to reach Dr. Chang with the other, but his phone was turned off. Sure, it might be unreasonable to ask him to meet her at the clinic at five in the morning, but what an exasperating man, turning off his phone at night when that was the nature of the his work meant being on call at all hours.

In the last half-dozen years, she'd stopped by the clinic if she caught a cold or needed a checkup, but she'd never been so seriously injured as to require Dr. Chang's emergency services. While it was partly because she could suture wounds that she could reach herself, it was also because her assignments tended to wrap up without complications, so much so that she found herself wondering if the ease with which she

dispatched her targets was due more to their carelessness than her still-sharp skills. Along with the fact
that fewer jobs came her way as the agency grew, she
suspected that she was assigned comparatively simple
jobs for some unknown reason, perhaps as a generous
consideration to a has-been or as a way to signal she
should retire already, but then again when she was out
in the field it was shocking how careless people were
about self-defense and how completely unprepared
they were. People who entrusted their safety to pro-
fessionals, people such as executives of major corporations driven around by assistants, and celebrities with
private security teams, tended to be relaxed and un-
guarded. Even if they had the most skilled bodyguard
right next to them, that lack of readiness rendered
all protective measures useless. People shared urban
legends that exaggerated society's chaos, such as how
foreigners kidnap people to harvest and smuggle their
organs, which corporations blamed for curbing the
culture of after-parties though it was really because of
the recession; sales of self-defense gadgets rose steadily,
but crime rates hadn't surged so dramatically as to indicate the end of the world. If, in the past, five out of
ten overnight incidents were reported in the newspapers, in today's hyperconnected media landscape
nine out of ten such incidents were brought to light.

Thanks to the twenty-four-hour news cycle, a single event would be repeatedly blasted out at least seven times in ten different media outlets. As the media fanned certain stories, whether for profit or to pull attention away from important political issues, people became desensitized by the repetition and let their guards down, making themselves vulnerable to danger until an even more shocking incident happened. Fundamentally, people didn't believe that they and their parents and siblings were unprepared. They were physically—and even more critically, mentally—prone to cracks and openings, as if they were a half-woven textile or a wide-open box.

Even if they are as unimpressive as dead leaves on the ground, have all of your skills at hand when you deal with them. If you think they are no competition and it'll be easy, the amount you didn't prepare will come back to bite you. Think of them as clients who hold your life and income in their hands.

Hornclaw forced herself to stay awake and gripped the steering wheel tightly. What happened was due to her carelessness, having dealt with unprepared fools for too long. The air in the car undulated from Ryu's admonishment, stabbing her scar-hardened memories. If she could just get herself home... She always kept a first-aid kit at the ready. But now all she could recall was that she kept it at the ready, not its actual location in her apartment. Despite the name she gave her, Deadweight was a rather useful and clever dog, so maybe even if she collapsed by the front door Deadweight would smell the blood and know to go fetch the first-aid kit. She wasn't sure if she would be able to sufficiently contort herself to clean the wound on her back and stay awake with a clear mind through it all, but she stepped harder on the gas, repeating the words *disinfectant, gauze, antibiotics, painkillers* to herself. This would never have become an issue before, when her veins were springy and taut and new blood roared continuously through them and her body was so resilient that she was like an apple that didn't bruise even after someone threw it against the ground. She would have stopped bleeding a long time ago and this wound would have been a mere scratch that wouldn't have fazed her at all, and this job itself wouldn't have been risky enough to draw blood to begin with… that is, *before*.

With about ten miles left, she arrived at an intersection and spotted a bright window on the third story of an old building by the boulevard, across the three-lane road by the market. She was at the clinic, and someone was there. It could be that someone had forgotten to turn off the light at the end of the day, but maybe Dr. Chang was treating another specialist and didn't realize that his phone was dead, and though all of this was a way for her to justify her mistakes, Hornclaw truly didn't have the energy to drive all the way home. She had barely managed to come all this way as it was, hanging on by a single spider silk of strength. She quickly parked and went into the building.

The elevator was on the third floor, and before she pushed the call button it began to descend. When the doors opened, she brushed past an old man coming out of the elevator, and because of the blood running down her back and filling the back of her shoes, she didn't think twice about the fact that someone was emerging from the building at this hour; in fact, she grew even more confident that Dr. Chang was at the clinic. The old man must be another specialist who had seen the doctor for an urgent appointment. But was there another specialist her age still working?

The clinic door was open a crack, through which she could see that the reception area and the waiting room were shrouded in darkness, but Room 3 was lit. As everything around her threatened to sink into oblivion, Hornclaw swung open the door, confident that she'd see Chang. Even if he wasn't here, there had to be something she could use to fix herself up.

"Dr. Chang."

A tall man in a white coat turned around, but he looked young, half Dr. Chang's age. Why was a contract doctor here at this hour? By the time she realized she had to get out of this place, the doctor was approaching her, asking, *Are you all right?* As she backed away the calendar on the wall shot up to the ceiling and the LED lights overhead tumbled to the floor and the young doctor's face rushed over as he shouted, his features contorting like a Munch painting before dissolving into nothing.

So this was the fatal blemish on her forty-five-year disease control career.

When she woke up, she found herself on her side and she felt pressure from the back of her neck to her waist. A bandage was wrapped around her wrist; she followed the long transparent line inserted there, which connected to a fluid, dripping sap-like, from an IV hanging above her head.

"How are you feeling?"

Only when she heard the cautious voice behind her did she realize that she was in Room 3. She flinched.

The doctor's hand pressed gently down on the sheet. "Please don't move. I dressed your wound and gave you some stitches. You were already unconscious so I didn't think you needed additional anesthesia.

You were bleeding heavily from cuts and a lacera-
tion, which is about six inches long, and that made
your clothes stick to you, so I had to cut them off. I
apologize for that."

The voice was clearly not Dr. Chang's. Partly as
a reflex and partly out of habit when she found herself in a situation where she might have to attack,
Hornclaw put a hand to her chest, but when she only
touched flesh instead of a blade, she more clearly understood her predicament. What she hadn't realized
earlier, since she could barely move, was that only a
thin sheet covered her bare body and that this man's
hand was on it; humiliation and confusion surged si-
multaneously from the depths of her chest. Her first
concern should have been how to silence this doctor,
who must have figured out who she was—perhaps he
didn't know exactly what she did but by cutting off
her clothes he would have seen her knives organized
by type in the inner pocket of her jacket and as long as
he wasn't a dummy he would have realized that something fishy was going on. But strangely her thoughts
didn't go there even though she wasn't groggy or all
that concerned about making trouble at a clinic with
which the agency had an agreement.

"I'm glad you made it here," the doctor continued.
"We might have needed to give you a blood transfu-

sion, but your clothes applied pressure on the wound and stopped the bleeding just in time. You got here right before a transfusion would have been necessary. It could have been very serious if you were just a little later... Oh, I'm sorry. Am I just saying the obvious?"

Her shoulder twitched, indicating that she wanted him to move his hand.

"Who are you!"

Normally she'd never speak so rudely to a complete stranger—in part because she rarely had reason to speak with anyone outside of the disease control community—but since she might have to kill this young man and he was probably more than suspicious of her identity, a terse tone was necessary to take control.

"The internist who works here every Wednesday and Friday?"

"Come around where I can see you."

She heard slippers dragging against the floor as the doctor came up to the chair in front of the cot and settled down. As she only ever saw Dr. Chang, she had no idea who this man was, and there was no way for her to know whether he'd worked here for a long time or was brand-new. He looked to be in his midthirties. At most in his late thirties. What a waste to have to eliminate this young man, Hornclaw thought as she squirmed under the sheet. The young doctor's expression was clear and gentle, and he looked like the type of person who would flip his pockets inside out and give everything he had to anyone begging and clinging on, but he was unexpectedly quick to understand the situation, as was made clear when he spoke.

"You don't have to look all over the place like that. I didn't call anyone. Nobody else is here."

Hornclaw fixed her nervous gaze on him. Instead of saying *Thanks, but why didn't you*, she looked up at the doctor's firm jaw without lowering her suspicion; maybe he wasn't a real doctor but was involved in something dubious; after all, he didn't call the authorities even after having looked in her pockets. She noticed that even the simple surgical instruments that would normally be laid around had been scrupulously put away. There were always a set of tweezers and dull scissors in the pencil holder on the desk, but even if she launched herself toward it right now, she didn't think she could get there in a single leap and grab them, not because she was in pain but because she was conscious of being naked, and she would probably end up pulling the sheet around her, wasting time and restricting her movements.

If you hesitate you could get caught. Everything you have, everything you are wearing, could be taken from you. In that situation, forget that you're a woman. Who's going to look at your body? Who has the presence of mind to do that? If there is even the smallest opportunity to flip the situation, do what you need to do, even if you have to be naked. If you fail it will be because of your lingering pride.

But such a situation Ryu spoke about had never happened, and she had never felt a serious threat to her life on any job. Over the years, she eventually stopped going to public baths, not wanting to reveal the scars and wounds on her body to strangers, and even in this very moment she knew, however faintly, that she wouldn't be free from the desperate urge to cover her body.

The doctor noted that she was constantly monitoring her surroundings. "I don't know what you're looking for, but I put all the sharp and dangerous things aside. I won't be able to face my boss if anything happens, so…"

At this point, whether he was a real or fake doctor he did seem like someone she could talk to honestly, but she didn't have any desire to reveal what kind of person she was, and even if she did she certainly wouldn't want to share life stories with this young doctor.

"Pretty smart for someone so young. Do you know who I am?"

He shrugged. "A patient?"

By then she'd already ripped off the bandage under her sheet and pulled out the needle, and in the next moment she reached out and yanked the glass IV bottle from its hook and slammed it down against the metal rails of the cot. The IV liquid and glass shards sprayed all over the room and the doctor raised an arm to shield his eyes, and in less than two seconds she had pushed the doctor against the wall, her arm pressing against his throat, the broken IV bottle aimed at his eye, all the while wrapped in the sheet, mindful as she was of her nudity.

"Listen up. Keep joking around and this will go straight into your brain. What's your deal? Go on. Start with why you're here at this hour."

She was aiming specifically at his eye, but as it was a section of the round bottle that she was holding, she could also sever the doctor's nose if she so chose.

"Your stitches...are going to pop."

He was so close to her that she would have heard even the smallest intake of breath, and in this space she smelled the delicate scent of his moisturizer mixed with antiseptic, which for some reason didn't make her feel ill or give her a headache. A friendly, kind, devoted tone like this, when his carotid artery was about to be slashed?

"Doesn't matter. Who are you?" She leaned harder on his neck.

"A doctor, I said. I'm here early because of my father, who sells fruit in the market over there. He's been going to work every day at the crack of dawn since it's leading up to Chuseok, and he said his back was hurting even more, so I got him X-rays and painkillers from the clinic before work. I used the clinic's resources for personal reasons, is what I'm saying."

That was when Hornclaw remembered the old man who got off the elevator earlier.

"What I'm trying to say is this. We both have something to hide, so maybe we don't need to tell anyone about what happened here. Do you agree? I don't care at all what it is that you do, and I really don't want to get fired for giving away medications."

Could she trust this man? How could she be sure that he won't say anything, even in passing, maybe to a nurse? She leaned a little harder into the doctor's neck, thinking of what might happen. She could just go after him later if he didn't keep his promise, but that would mean her career would be over. Depending on how it went down, she would be unlikely to survive. She weighed the life of the man under her arm and all the other consequences.

Hornclaw finally let go and shoved him aside, causing the doctor to hit his shoulder against the desk and crumple to the floor. She stood in front of the coughing doctor as he straightened his clothes and threatened him, still holding the IV bottle. "Forget everything you saw here today. You saw nothing and nothing happened."

"Yes, I got it. I for one didn't come here until my shift began. You can put that down now, you know."

She wasn't about to put the bottle down before she could throw on some clothes and get out of there. "Internists aren't supposed to stitch people up, are they? Do you always commit malpractice when you see someone bleeding?"

"Of course not. I did it because it was an emergency, and it didn't come out very nicely. It will probably leave a scar. You might want to wait a week to bathe, and it'll take about two months for the stitches to dissolve." The doctor checked the time and began to tidy up, as if he really did want to get out of the clinic before the nurses arrived.

Hornclaw felt a little more at ease and more trusting; in her years of work she'd developed an instant suspicion toward strangers and honed a keen sense of someone's honesty, and this doctor wasn't showing any animosity toward her, who turned on him and attacked after he saved her life. In fact, he was placidly indifferent, having only performed what was required of him as a doctor, even if the way he'd done it wasn't quite aboveboard.

She tossed the bottle fragment on the bed and looked out the window. It was after six thirty and people were beginning their days, and as the building was by a market there were more people outside than in a residential area. What should she do? She could make it to her car with the sheet around her, but since she then had to drive home she wasn't keen on doing anything that might catch someone's attention in the few seconds she got in and out of the car. There would be a few hospital gowns in the X-ray exam room, but only tops.

She spotted two paper bags next to the desk. One contained the clothes that had been cut off her body, and the other held hurriedly selected new clothes in drab black and gray, similar to what she'd been wearing.

"I went to the market while you were sleeping," the young doctor explained. "I don't know if these are okay, but I chose clothes similar to yours."

"Prepared, aren't you? How much is it?" Hornclaw quickly put on the new outfit as the doctor turned to sweep the shards off the floor.

"They weren't much. It's on me."

"I get that you're embarrassed to ask for money, but that won't do. If you keep insisting I'll just leave you what I want to pay for it, including for this visit."

She heard him let out a laugh.

"All right, then. I'll use it to buy my daughter ice cream."

Hornclaw paused while shoving her arm through a shirtsleeve, the word "daughter" melting like ice cream along the outer edge of her ear. She quickly buttoned her shirt and took the bag of old clothes. "Thanks."

"Wait." The doctor reached up to the top of the tall bookcase and pulled something out. "You almost forgot." He held out her tools, sealed in a sterile bag.

She yanked the bag out of his hands. "What did you do with these?"

"Are you worried I cooked with them? I just cleaned and sterilized them."

"If you do anything…" She didn't finish her sentence about how she would cut or drown him. She would probably never cross paths with him again. She closed the door behind her and ran down the stairs, clutching her chest to calm her shallow breathing.

After cleaning up the mess and getting ready to leave, the doctor would have noticed four crisp fifty-thousand-won bills partly slid under the keyboard, and whether he imagined his daughter's joy at receiving an unexpected present or he shook his head at the old lady's unnecessary act, she thought he would have most definitely smiled. Hornclaw gripped the steering wheel, wondering what that smile looked like, feeling faint; she shook her head a few times, thinking it was probably the blood loss.

After her regular checkup with Dr. Chang, Hornclaw stops by the traditional market next to the clinic. A clear dome tops the narrow alleys, and it's not quite a traditional market anymore, with each stall modernized and the signs made uniform, all lined up in dry objectivity, erasing any lingering nostalgia she used to feel when she wandered through old markets; in fact, if she bought a bag of bean sprouts and asked for a discount or an extra handful, she might be met with glares, especially as this market even has a supermarket in the center. There are signs and ads about sales and free gifts to celebrate the opening plastered everywhere, and the size of the supermarket and the goods sold there are similar to other big-box stores even though the name isn't that of a chain. Hornclaw doesn't know why there's a supermarket here, when there are already numerous produce stalls, dried fish sellers and mills. She does know that the purveyors in the market opposed the big-box store, which is now under construction about a mile away. Since the supermarket is teeming with shoppers, maybe its opening here is a tactic to draw customers to the traditional market and put up a fight against the big-box store.

Anyway, Hornclaw walks past a stall selling black goat medicinal products and pauses in front of a fruit seller; the owner she's seen frequently must be out for delivery, as his wife, limping, stands up to greet her. After a moment of hesitation, Hornclaw asks if she has any peaches.

To be fully prepared for any eventuality, Hornclaw easily learned the name of the young doctor who treated her that night and the location of his parents' store. The doctor's last name is Kang. Kang and Chang. Chang and Kang. When she burst into the clinic in the middle of the night, it must have been after the nurse slipped Dr. Kang's name plate into the acrylic holder before the end of the previous workday, and because of the amount of blood she lost, she'd been losing consciousness and hadn't noticed the subtle difference in the names.

No matter what excuse she comes up with, she's fully aware that she committed a serious error, nearly blowing her cover—sure, she hadn't revealed her actual job and the name of the agency, but the core of who she is had been made clear, and if he hadn't decided to look the other way she would have found herself in a dicey spot. The agency would certainly hear about it if Dr. Kang decided to report what happened in Room 3 that night; she didn't really believe the young doctor would keep his word. Hornclaw has enough affection for this work that she doesn't want to retire with her reputation tanked, and while affection is a strange way to describe it, she feels connected to the work as if by an umbilical cord. An umbilical cord that manages barely to provide just enough nutrition before suddenly wrapping itself around your neck, choking you to death.

The shopkeeper pulls out a box of the juiciest-looking white peaches for Hornclaw. "It's pure sugar, I'm telling you. It just melts in your mouth. You don't even have to chew!"

The box holds twelve peaches.

Hornclaw shakes her head. "That's far too many. I just need four."

Actually, she only needs two, since she would have one and give one to Deadweight, but Hornclaw figures the shopkeeper wouldn't want to sell so few peaches. Well, she and Deadweight will just have to eat two each.

"Just four? How small is the family? These last longer than you might think. You can take your time eating them." Even as she says that, the shopkeeper puts four in a plastic bag and holds it out before pausing and adding one more, her movements natural and gentle.

Hornclaw selects clean bills with which to pay and looks at the shopkeeper's face—at the woman's faded, trembling eyelashes. That continuous spasm marks chronic fatigue and lack of minerals, and based on the way the woman is sweating despite the chill of the unheated shop, Hornclaw can tell that she is in ill health. The woman reminds Hornclaw of all mothers' universal sacrifice, the way they can devote their entire being to their children's education without looking after themselves, often pushing through with the help of painkillers. However, this woman's child clearly didn't enjoy the success his parents would have wanted for him, as he isn't a professor at a university hospital and he hasn't opened his own practice. In any case, this is an unusual shopping experience, as it's rare for a shopkeeper to be this generous during a recession and amid the ongoing demolition of traditional markets, adding an extra peach in her bag even though she bought not eight or even six but merely four. The seemingly indifferent Dr. Kang might take after his mother, in the way he treated a patient outside his specialty and even bought her new clothes.

Right then, the owner of the shop pulls up on his bicycle and manages just barely to stay upright, hitting Hornclaw's bag in the process. "Oh my, I'm so sorry."

His wife scolds him. "I told you to stop riding it if you can't keep your balance. Do you know what happens these days when you damage a woman's bag? A bag can go for several million won, you clumsy man."

"Does it look like I did it on purpose?"

As the couple bickers, Hornclaw wonders if she should say her bag is a twenty-five-thousand-won fake, but then her eyes are drawn to a young girl the man lifts off the back of the bicycle.

"Grandma!" the girl calls out, running into the stall. She is wearing a yellow backpack printed with the name and phone number of her kindergarten. "Grandpa's really bad at riding the bike. I don't ever want to ride it again."

"Haeni, I didn't mean it," her grandmother soothes. "There's no other way. It's too far to walk, right? Ride with Grandpa even if it's a little shaky, all right?"

"I'll ride in Daddy's car!"

"Daddy's busy, you know that. Today he goes to this clinic, tomorrow he goes to the other one..."

The girl pouts. Dr. Kang's daughter. What flavor ice cream did she get that day? Or maybe he bought her a pretty outfit. They say kids' clothes are ridiculously expensive these days, so maybe what she left wasn't enough. Hornclaw smiles when she spots a small, cute mole on the girl's jaw. Everything wondrous and mysterious in the universe is contained in this one little girl. Is this a natural sentiment to have when gazing at a young girl, even though she's an old woman who's never had a grandchild? The way it isn't just people who live by the shore that revere the ocean? What she's feeling is a sense of wonder toward a being who is out of reach and the objectification of an unfulfilled emotion.

"Her mom must be busy, too," Hornclaw murmurs as if to herself, and feels a twinge of guilt; she already knows that Dr. Kang's wife is dead. But most neighborhood women her age would naturally insert themselves right about now, asking where the mom is while grandpa picks up the child. This is how she puts on the act of a regular old busybody, pretending to suffer from an empty nest and making small talk with people her age.

"Her mom is in heaven."

"Oh... I'm so sorry. I shouldn't have said anything," Hornclaw says, feigning surprise and pulling her hat lower over her forehead. If she was more of a chatterbox she would interject, *How sad, at such a young age!* assuming that she must have been young even though she would have no idea, breezing over the other person's pain to satisfy her own curiosity, but she can't quite bring herself to do that.

"No, no. It happened a long time ago. Something went wrong when this one was born at the big university hospital. That's how her mom went. She was far too young. She didn't have a serious disease or anything like that."

The woman's voice retains her outrage from that time, and Hornclaw listens quietly as she is familiar with people of a certain age who tell their whole life story to a complete stranger at Pagoda Park or on the subway, saying that they could write an entire book about it.

"How could she go like that when her husband is a doctor?" the shopkeeper continues. "He was completely devastated and caused a scene. His coworkers just pulled him away and shut him up. So useless. Was anyone asking for compensation? Was anyone asking for punishment? Of course not. We're all human. It could easily have been him in that situation. All he wanted was an apology, and they still ignored him. So in the end the surgeon or the professor or whoever it is calls him up and you know what he says? 'Everyone who wants a huge settlement always says all they wanted was a heartfelt apology.' Can you believe that? How dare they? So insulting. And so that's why he's done with university hospitals, and instead works part-time at this clinic and that clinic. At least he didn't try to end it all, because of his daughter."

"That must have been so hard," Hornclaw says. "It can't be easy for you to mind the store and take care of your granddaughter. If it's been that long it might be time…" She realizes how insensitive she sounds and stops speaking. She's nearly blurted out that it's time for him to get married again, right in front of the girl, who's looking up curiously at Hornclaw as she speaks; though she isn't being intentionally malicious, she's being nosy beyond belief.

But the shopkeeper understands what Hornclaw was beginning to say. "Well, nobody is all that interested, since he's not a dentist or a plastic surgeon and makes next to nothing. And he doesn't even have his own practice. She's not a baby anymore and we're just shopkeepers—who would be interested? Young people these days care about that kind of thing, you know. He's a doctor, but what good does it do?"

Her husband, who was tying down a box of apples on the back of his bicycle, interrupts. "Enough with the complaining! Why are you delaying the customer?"

Embarrassed, the shopkeeper nudges the girl off

her lap and opens the cash register to count out the change. "Oh, I'm sorry. Now that I'm old, I just keep chatting and chatting."

"Not at all," Hornclaw reassured. "All I have is time. I do the same thing." She says this even though she doesn't tell her life story to anyone else, not sometimes, not ever.

The girl flings her backpack on the ground and bows deeply to Hornclaw, saying goodbye. The name Kang Haeni is written on a label by the straps. Hornclaw looks down at the lovable little girl, whose features are cute and small. She must take after her mother; it's not immediately obvious that she is Dr. Kang's daughter.

"How old are you, princess?"

"I'm six."

Six. Hornclaw already knew, but now that she hears how the girl says it, it feels as though she would remember the child's babyish pronunciation forever, the moisture in her words never evaporating.

"Be good to your grandma and grandpa. See you later." Hornclaw turns to go, looking away from the half-torn price tag poking out of the back of the child's shirt, an oversight by her father or grandparents. She won't mention to anyone the sensation she felt when she left Room 3 a month ago, a sensation that felt awfully like dizziness, and she won't let herself remember that feeling as she looks down at this small girl. She won't think about the moment she briefly forgot about the flesh and blood and bone fragments that formed her world and, letting her guard down, dreamed of happy possibilities; she won't recall the fingers that carefully picked up the pieces of the IV bottle or the forgiving smile tinged with the smell of antiseptic. The faint murmur in her heart was the product of her fantasy, and she immediately regretted indulging in it.

As she walks away, Hornclaw takes out a peach and brings it up to her nose. The thin skin, blushing at the top near the stem in a gradation of pink and white, feels like velvet, and the soft fuzz doesn't mute the sweet scent, which gradually erases the bitter aftertaste of her smile.

An old man, perched on a tilted stool in front of a blood sausage restaurant by the subway station, is glowering in her direction, so Hornclaw holds the peach out to him. To put it charitably, the old man is dressed like a wandering poet, and he shows up at the market from time to time, getting free food from several eateries. Perhaps he doesn't remember how to get home or maybe he used to live around here. The police or a middle-aged couple who seem to be family frequently show up to collect him, but he comes back again to wander the area as if nothing happened.

She holds out the peach only because it happens to be in her hand when their eyes meet and it feels more awkward to put it back in the bag, and in fact she does consider the possibility that he might refuse the offering since she is essentially treating him like a beggar. The old man gazes at the peach and, without a word or gesture of any kind, takes it and immediately chomps down on it. The peel and flesh are crushed between the old man's teeth, some of which are missing, and before she turns to go she watches a perfect small world being smashed inside his mouth as the juices run down his face and along his wrist.

The aroma lingering in her mouth without having tasted the peach; the scent of the sugary, sticky nectar, so sweet that it stings—she locks it all in her heart, not easily visible, like a small new leaf sprouting on a tree.

The boy, who had just returned home from his after-school program where he studied logic, essay writing and philosophy, purportedly to cultivate leadership, was taking out his key when something heavy crashed, boom, against the inside of the thick steel door. Then came the sound of something sliding down and landing on the floor with a thump.

His mother had left for a two-week academic conference overseas and the only person at home right now would be the temp housekeeper, and there was still a week before they were to move; had the movers already come and were throwing boxes and furniture around? At night? Puzzled, the boy accidentally dropped his keys, breaking the sparkly keychain with his initials on it. *We should get a keypad lock at the new apartment*, he thought. He managed to unlock the door and pull it open, though it felt heavier than usual, as if a big planter was leaning against it.

As the door opened, out spilled a slumped body onto the boy's feet. He looked down at his father's head. His father's eyes were open, but dark red blood trickled from the top of his head down between his eyes in half a dozen paths. Blood lapped at the boy's feet and along the hallway as a puddle began to form and the smell of blood filled the boy's nose, but strangely, even as he thought, *This is blood*, he was suddenly reminded of maple syrup poured over hot, fluffy pancakes instead of the metallic smell of death commonly accompanying a bloodbath. So it was that strange association that made him gaze down at his father's head, lying on top of his own feet like a vanitas still life, instead of fleeing, and he couldn't figure out how death could emit such a sweet, comforting scent; his sense of reality had sloughed off like dead skin cells.

By the time he looked into the apartment, nobody was there; the hallway to the living room seemed to loll like a dead person's tongue as the evening breeze drifted in. The boy heard the door to the veranda sliding open in the living room, and when he understood

that the sound was being made by the person responsible for what happened to his father, hot urine trickled down his pants into his shoes. Figuring it could be
helpful to the police if he saw who it was even from far
away, the boy quickly pushed his father's head aside,
which he hadn't been able to bring himself to do until
just then, and rushed into the living room.

What he saw first was a pearl-hued back, then a
scarf draped over an open-backed shirt, the moon-
light illuminating the person's hard spine and shoulder blades, poised to sprout wings. The killer was
perched on the veranda window frame and turned to
look sideways, calmly, at the boy, and the instant he
recognized her as the housekeeper who'd been helping out for the last six days, he forgot everything he
should have remembered—that she was in her early-
to midforties, thin, short and with straight, shoulder-length hair—and was caught in an illusion that
the breeze around her was bringing in a scattering of
flower petals. Here, the boy was genuinely curious:
how do you not have even a single drop of blood on
you when my father looks like that? How did you do
that? Maybe she wasn't the one who did it.

Right before she jumped out of the window it
seemed like she said something, but the boy couldn't
hear; her body seemed to be pumping out chilly air

and howling wind. After a while, he remembered that they were on the fourth floor; he slowly dragged his sludgy feet toward the veranda, fearful that as soon as he looked down, her hand would shoot out, grab him by the ankles and throw him into the air. A long while had passed by the time he dared to peep out, and of course nobody was there; he saw only the marks of chain ropes along the side of the building.

This was when the woman who lived across the hall came home, and when the elevator doors opened, she spotted the sprawled body and the bloodbath in the hallway and screamed as the doors closed quickly again. By now sitting on the living room floor, the boy didn't hear the sirens approaching as he mulled over what the housekeeper had said to him—maybe she'd said, "Forget this." A few officers entered gingerly, holding their breath, and when they found small bloody footsteps leading into the living room they leaped in, yelling "Don't move!" But when they found not a murderer but a boy staring out the window in a daze, a puddle of piss and blood all around him, they shouted, "There's a kid!" and wrapped him in a scratchy blanket they found who knows where. The pilled blanket was dusty and the dust floated in the air, mixing with the white flower petals and pollen from the outside and leaving behind a musty smell.

The prosecutors began investigating the victim's residential construction business, beginning with the development plans for an apartment complex and extending all the way to the approvals, and uncovered more than seven inconsistencies, including flaws in the scale of construction and incomplete processes overseen by various agencies, and, more gravely, evidence that a request to alter zoning categories at the beginning of construction had been illegitimately approved. The officials who violated regulations and accepted bribes were fired or sent to prison, which helped the prosecutors' win rate. As it would have been more practical and effective to go through the legal system to punish the boy's father for what he'd done, even if it took longer, it didn't make sense that his actions would have caused his death. The prosecutors thoroughly investigated potential grudges against the boy's father, such as whether he had funneled work to certain subcontractors, or unilaterally broken contracts, or maintained unfair deals. They examined whether he made power plays that could have triggered a hit, but the victim's dealings actually revealed his innate obsequiousness toward people in power; there was no real evidence that he bullied weaker parties.

The natural next step was to dig into his private life, but there was no indication that he was engaged in some illicit affair; however, he had paid for several hundred one-night stands at certain bars. Six of the girls they could identify had died from illness or overdose around the time of the murder, but none of their deaths seemed to be related to the killing. Later, on a TV program about unsolved crimes, a psychiatrist, who was featured with his voice disguised, raised suspicions about the calm, cold smile and flat demeanor of the victim's thirteen-year-old son, but his implications were widely condemned.

Based on information provided by the boy's mother, who rushed home from the conference as soon as she heard what happened, the temp housekeeper was the prime suspect, but nobody could figure out her true identity or motive. The boy's mother had used one particular agency, but as she hired help irregularly, a different person had shown up each time, and this last time the mother had been in such a hurry that she hadn't even personally met the housekeeper. The family registration certificate and the copy of the ID on file were fake, and the photo didn't match the boy's description. The temp agency was fined and closed for its negligence, and the CEO was investigated, but no links to the victim were found. While the investigation proceeded, conjecture abounded, but nothing more. The victim's projects were put on hold, then sold off to other entities, and the boy was admitted to a psych ward for half a year. People gradually forgot about the incident. The boy never managed to have a good relationship with his mostly absent mother, whose relatives soon introduced her to a new man, a foreign biologist.

There was one thing the boy never mentioned to anyone. When he helped create the composite sketch he'd told the authorities that he wasn't entirely sure what the perpetrator looked like or what she wore, since they had just passed each other by in the mornings and evenings, but the truth was that he had looked into her face many times, up close. Following his mother's written directions, the housekeeper had made sure he took three types of allergy medication, each of which had to be administered in varying doses and intervals. In fact there had been a request: "He can't swallow pills so please grind them into powder using the mortar and pestle in the cupboard," which must have been a burdensome task for someone without nursing experience, but the housekeeper had carefully sorted the medications each time and wordlessly ground them. As he gulped down the powder, he would look up at her face for a long time, fighting the urge to reach out and touch her soft, straight hair, which was so unlike his mother's perfectly blown-out do, all of which meant that no matter how intense his shock there was no way he could forget what she looked like.

The boy never found out why his father met such a grisly fate, but is now certain he knows the identity of the person who killed him.

There must have been people who had it out for his father, a self-made man who worked hard and clandestinely built a network with an eye toward entering politics. Today he knew that the housekeeper had merely completed her assignment, and that she generally didn't ask a single question when carrying out these jobs. Even if he asked her now why she'd killed his father she wouldn't know the answer; even if she had known back then exactly why her assignment was given to her, twenty years had now passed, and she likely wouldn't remember. Her nails had slashed far too many people.

The boy—now a thirty-three-year-old man—prefers the phrase "disease control" instead of "elimination."

Delivered gifts are generally received at the front desk, and the chief secretary checks the contents before bringing them into the chairman's office. A sealed envelope containing a letter or documents usually accompanies each gift, and after the assistants determine that the envelope is safe to open, it's sent straight in with the gift. Of course, in the case of cash, it doesn't tend to come in an envelope; usually money arrives in an apple crate or, if they are trying to be more thoughtful, a Samsonite. With USB drives, the chief secretary checks them for viruses or malware first on his personal laptop, and in doing so tends to see their contents, which is why a discreet relative always serves as the chairman's chief secretary.

Of the gifts that enter the chairman's office, most are returned to the chief secretary's desk for the staff to divvy up, including, on occasion, brand-name goods, to the delight of the assistants.

"Someone is here to see you on behalf of Chairman Lee from J Pharmaceutical Company."

"Send him in."

When the chairman says "send him in" like today, instead of "he can leave it with you," one of the assistants invites in the messenger who, in this case, is carrying a large fruit basket, but fruit could be stacked on top of layers of cash or drugs. It's not for the chief secretary to raise concerns when he doesn't recognize the visitor. Following strict protocol, he asks the messenger to raise his arms, then glides a metal detector wand from the messenger's armpits to his knees and around the fruit basket, even though he knows the messenger would have gone through the same precautions in the lobby downstairs, before bowing. "Sorry for the inconvenience."

The messenger nods, smiling generously to signal that he knows the chief secretary is just doing his job. An assistant shows him to the chairman's office; his stride is elegant and poised, and the assistant feels they had been rude for searching him. He's taller and more handsome than the chief secretary of J Pharmaceutical, and wearing horn-rimmed Paul Smith glasses and a Hugo Boss suit. Judging from his straight posture and confident gait, he seems accustomed to these types of errands—it's not altogether odd for companies to hire someone specifically for shady or unpleasant deals so that they won't be caught in the act.

The chairman glances at the fruit basket placed on the coffee table and goes back to reviewing the document in front of him. "Have a seat. I'm almost done," he says without looking up.

Hearing the messenger settle on the leather sofa, the chairman continues. "You're ten minutes early. Chairman Lee must have told you my schedule is tight, down to the second. When I met you at the club that time, you seemed well-mannered…"

The chairman raises his head now, but nobody is sitting on the sofa. He blinks, confused, and in that brief second the messenger is behind him; the chairman can't breathe, even before he perceives that there is pressure on his thyroid cartilage. Instinctively the chairman's hands shoot up toward his throat, but the taut wire digs more forcefully into his flesh. The chairman extends a trembling hand toward the emergency alarm installed below his desk, but the messenger's foot lands on the hand, pinning it to the arm of the chair. A bone snaps in the chairman's hand and the scream in his throat is swallowed, blocked by the pressure applied to his windpipe. The chairman scrabbles at his neck, trying to get hold of the wire, but there's no gap, not even for a fingernail. He launches his other hand behind him but the wire is long; he can't grab the messenger or his clothes. He bucks, trying to force the messenger to lose his grip, but the man behind him is bracing against the chairman's weight, hanging on to the wire. When the chair slides to the side, the chairman kicks futilely in the air, unable to make contact with his desk, and as hard as he tries to roll off the chair or tip it over, he can't; he's pinned in place. His shoes slide around on the plush carpet; his assistants on the other side of his heavy hardwood door don't have any clue as to what's transpiring inside. At any moment an assistant might knock on the door at any moment, wondering why the chairman hasn't requested tea for the guest. The messenger yanks on the wire and something severs in the chairman's spine; his head rolls forward while his body remains seated in the chair. The messenger brings a finger to the chairman's nose to check if he's breathing, then collects the wire and picks up the fruit basket. He slips his feet back into his shoes, which he'd left on the outer edge of the carpet.

The light on the intercom blinks. If the button is pressed, the assistant will ask, "Would you like some tea?" If there is no answer, someone will surely come in to check. The messenger enters the chairman's personal elevator within his office and presses the close button, hearing an assistant knock from outside. All the other floors are deactivated; it's a straight shot down to the underground parking lot. He hears screams down the elevator shaft as he laces his shoes with the wire.

When he gets out in the parking lot, he sees the chairman's driver polishing the limousine. Hearing the chairman's personal elevator open even though he didn't get a call from upstairs, the driver looks behind him, surprised, and that's when the messenger punches him, first in the temple and then the clavicle. The driver crumples to the ground as the phone rings in the booth. It would be a call from the chairman's office. With his elbow the messenger hits the button to open the automatic gate and walks out into the busy street. The police arrive fifteen minutes later, by which time he's walked a block away, hailed a cab and left. Within the corporation they quietly begin a preliminary investigation, keeping reporters at bay, as is usually the case for the killing of a powerful, influential man.

Disease control usually unfolds this way. You don't ask who wants what or why. Nobody explains why someone has become an insect that needs to be eliminated or why someone is now a rat that needs to be rousted. You don't need some Kafkaesque interpretation of how a person, gradually over a long period of time, or sometimes suddenly overnight, becomes vermin. The more high-ranking and powerful a client is and the more the target is someone with influence, the more the "why's" are left out when a disease control specialist comes on board. The request is often conveyed through a third party, so you don't even know who hired you. The disease control specialist doesn't think about who benefits when the target is excised or what is to be gained when someone dies. Only later, when you see the stock market react or the culture respond, do you begin to guess who the client is and why they hired you for the job, which is how most conspiracy theories germinate, but even then, all you have left is conjecture.

That is the kind of thing that had happened to his father long ago.

As it is with matchmaking, so it is with disease control. The client and the target are graded, like in a butcher shop, depending on their social position and influence, plus the complexities of the assignment, and the fee is determined through a mathematical formula. For less important clients the specialist could have several meetings, discussing possible methods and exchanging thoughts about the various problems that may crop up in the process. In jobs that allow for such personal meetings you are generally dealing with illicit affairs or grudges, which means you have to listen to the client's complaints. Some clients like this tend to talk in a roundabout way to justify their actions, while others, often the superwealthy, just toss a picture of the target at you and snap, "Take care of it." The specialists generally prefer to take on high-paying gigs, but they also like easy jobs, so they don't always mind the emotional labor of murmuring sympathies as the clients sob and vent. In his first few years in this line of work, it was a fun diversion to witness the clients' strange obsessions, regrets and rage as they put their lives on the line over trivial offenses, but their stories quickly grew monotonous and frustrating. Lately he's been focusing on work like today's, where there's no need to ask or answer any questions.

Then as now, there are always people who want to get rid of someone. While more and more specialists are entering the profession, a limited number of businesses specialize in disease control; at the agency, some specialists who aren't getting regular jobs freelance on the side, siphoning off clients and sometimes competing with the agency. A few years ago, the agency began to bring in more mid- to lower-level clients through the use of freelancers, assigning those jobs to the lowest bidder. The circumstances of the client and the target are noted in detail, accompanied by a star-rating system that notes the prominence and difficulty of the job. Specialists who want an easy target and quick money bid against each other to nab the assignment. As the client's fees remain the same, the bidding system potentially compromises quality, but those without a network or a reliable source of income tend to keep competing for these less-important gigs.

For a business built on discretion, it's only a matter of time before this unwieldy band puts the company in jeopardy—although the agency is widely known within the underground economy, it would still be a huge problem if their work became known to the pub-

lic—but such are Director Sohn's crass tactics. Bullfight smirks; he doesn't care what ends up happening
to Director Sohn. What is it to him if Sohn squan-
ders human resources this way, ruining the reputation
built up by the prior director? Let him get merged
with some errand services company in the outskirts
of the city.

The agency's main computer hard drive contained
data related to the last fifteen years of disease control.
The vow that the agency would destroy all documents after the completion of a job was just a sales
pitch; in fact, since you never knew when a client
might stab you in the back, these files, along with
voice and video recordings, were always saved in case
they needed to be used later as blackmail. Many documents were from jobs for which the statute of limi-
tations had expired but could still be incriminating
in the court of public opinion; as such, they were a
double-edged sword, information that could ensnare
both the client and the agency.

When you're ruined, you should hold hands and
tumble into hell together, Bullfight thought to himself one night as he slowly cracked the multiple layers
of passwords protecting the folders and sifted through

the contents, glancing periodically over at Worryfixer's sleeping form on the sofa.

Director Sohn didn't believe in keeping the hard drive in a portable safe, secluded in some random vacation home in the mountains. He believed in keeping it close by. The theory was that if prosecutors burst in on them to seize documents, it would be easier to pull out the hard drive and smash it right then and there. Because of this, Bullfight was able to flip through all the documents at his leisure after serving ginger tea spiked with a sleeping pill to Worryfixer for their bronchitis. They had asked him to wake them up in ten minutes but were out for three hours, and when they finally managed to rouse themself they even apologized for having made him stay in the office the whole time, watching over them.

Information about jobs over fifteen years old wasn't stored digitally. Those handwritten documents had to be in the filing cabinet. Bullfight took the bundle of keys from the inner pocket of Worryfixer's jacket and slotted each one in the cabinet, and when none of the seven fit, he tried each of the four smaller keys in the metal desk drawers. One unlocked the second drawer, and when he pushed aside tissues and staplers and other junk and tapped the bottom, it sounded like there was a hidden compartment under the particleboard, just as he suspected, and he pried it open to find yet another ring with more than forty keys hanging from it. Only about half were labeled, ranging from a key to a long-gone company car to the old office key. Bullfight glanced over at Worryfixer, exasperated by their incompetence, and then thinking about how Director Sohn operated, he began to shove the labeled keys into the keyhole of the cabinet; finally, the one labeled Madam's Closet opened it.

Closet? Whose clothes were these supposed to be, anyway?

It was a mess inside. Sure, there were old documents, but they were not organized alphabetically or by year; it seemed like someone had been flustered and stuffed them in chaotically. Listening to Worryfixer rustling in their sleep, he picked out some files and dusted them off.

Documents created sixteen to twenty-five years ago were typed with primitive software on a 286 or 386 computer, but since none of the specs were compatible with modern machines and there were no longer any floppy disk drives, he had to review thick documents printed on dot matrix or early-model inkjet printers. Going back further than twenty-five years ago, documents were typed using manual typewriters on coarse paper or written by hand; even worse, there were documents written in Chinese characters or in Japanese, with only the particles in Korean. After careful examination, tracing each line with his finger, Bullfight found the documents related to his father among the yellowed inkjet printouts.

What do I do with you now?

Bullfight thinks about Hornclaw's short fingernails, rough and cracked and chipped due to years of aggressive physical activity.

They would become prettier if he pulled them out, one by one, causing flower petals to bloom at the tip of each finger. Showier. There's no such thing in the world as a red that is prettier than blood, even if it turns brown when oxidized. A red that is deep and cruel, precisely because it turns murky.

He never daydreamed of acting out the plot of some third-rate martial arts novel, of finding the woman who bashed in his father's head and exacting revenge. His family wasn't the warm and fuzzy type, but it was still his family. In spite of that day being traumatic, he became a disease control specialist through his own volition; though volition made it sound like it was part of a grand plan, whereas, more truthfully, he ended up falling into this job. Not a lot of things in his life were inevitable. He didn't have a desperate, otherworldly desire to do this work, driven to resolve his baggage with other baggage. It wasn't that he especially loved getting rid of people, but as he didn't have a strong sense of morality that told him he couldn't possibly be in the same line of work as the woman who'd killed his father, he somehow—truly, just somehow—ended up doing this work. Most of what happened was a collage, created by the shapes and layers of unimportant events. His life was a totality of somehows.

Although he didn't hunt down the person who ordered the killing that day, he figured he might at one point or another come across a clue. If there was a reason not to be too curious about the woman who'd jumped out of the window, it was because he didn't expect her to still be alive to this day. Even if she was alive she would be over sixty, and if he found himself face-to-face with a wrinkled elderly woman, an even larger piece of him would crumble. No matter how small the industry was, there were a lot of specialists out there—how could he expect to find someone who knew what happened to her?—and he didn't want to put in the effort to track her down only to hear that she'd died in a botched assignment.

Still, when he discovered that some of his father's files had been destroyed, he was disappointed. When he searched the client who ordered the hit he found that there were over three thousand people with the

same name, and he couldn't find anything related to
the killing. It seemed likely that the client was working for someone else, and there was no evidence as
to the reason his father was targeted. The event was
buried beneath layers of context and baked like a pas-
try, and by the time he dug down deep everything
had been eaten. But if there was one thing he gleaned
from the file, it was that she was still alive and that
she was, in fact, currently active.

Bullfight began to frequent the office, choosing
to receive and deliver the results of his assignments
in person.

What should I say to you?

The instant Bullfight saw her, he immediately recognized her graceful eyebrows, sunken cheeks and
obstinate lips, but of course she looked obliviously at
him, shaking off his greeting. *We don't need to get to
know each other,* she said. *There's no teamwork required
and I'm not the kind of person who would be beneficial for
you to know.*

He wasn't altogether surprised that she didn't remember, but a sound like a pill bottle rattling sur-
faced from somewhere deep inside. Scenes that formed
his shattered past lurched and rushed past behind his
eyelids.

What should I do to you?

She was already old and stubborn and far from wise. When she turned her head indifferently like that, he could reach out, grab her skull and bash it in. Does she have her guard up? Would she be able to block or evade his attack? It won't be easy. She knew very well that her body wouldn't be able to live up to her will.

Even so, it would be a disappointment if she sat there pathetically like all the other pitiful bastards, bidding lower and lower.

A woman who smashed his father's head open couldn't be relegated to doing sad jobs like that. That, at the very least, couldn't be the story.

He had unknowingly stretched his hand toward her back; he withdrew it and brought it to his lips, observing her. Instead of the straight hair he'd wanted to wrap around his fingers as a boy, she now had wavy, brittle gray hair, puffy like a ball of dust on an unreachable shelf. This was the reality at odds with his memory, a sensation that would forever remain as an absence.

Bullfight emerges from the taxi. It's springtime and the temperature has fluctuated dramatically since morning, so he's forced to take off his jacket. Suddenly, out of the blue, he has a craving for something sweet; the urge is so strong that he's taken aback, and it's a little different from hunger rumbling the stomach. It's a compulsion, an impatience that demands immediate gratification. He rummages through his pockets where he finds only empty chocolate wrappers; he's about to flick them to the ground but, spotting a street cleaner in a light green uniform, he stuffs them back in.

He doesn't come across a single convenience store, so he takes a white peach out of the fruit basket covered by his jacket and brings it unthinkingly to his mouth. The soft fuzz tickles his lips and a rash blooms around his mouth not long after his first bite. Overflowing juice trickles down his chin and drips along the lines of his palm, pooling on the band of his Rolex before tracing a sticky line down his arm and dampening his rolled-up shirtsleeve. He licks the sweetness off his lips, intensifying the itchiness. Bullfight doesn't just drop the nearly whole fruit on the ground or in a trash can, but instead throws it as hard as he can against the ground. Smashed bits of fruit splatter onto a stray cat and the animal shrinks away, and, settling at a distance, begins to groom itself.

Sometimes he was curious about one thing from his time with the housekeeper. Why did she bother giving him the correct medication, prepared with such care? If she wanted to, she could have easily tampered with them; it would have been so simple to get rid of a mere child. Was it to adhere to the principle of not harming anyone who isn't a target? It would have been more work to stick to that mandate; nobody would have known if she took whatever she wanted, ground it up, mixed it with flour and gave it to him.

"Ugh. It's so hot."

Instead of irritation and laziness, his waterlogged words are tinged with a slight excitement.

When she's given a new assignment, which happens
once every other month or so, she'll finish her prep-
arations and, on the morning of the job, she'll kneel
and pull Deadweight close to her as if she's perform-
ing a religious ceremony.

She often forgets to feed or bathe her, and she rarely
walks her, but the dog appears not to mind her lifestyle. Their relationship seems like that of your average
dog and owner, but as they met later in life, neither
shows too much affection, and while Deadweight
runs to the front door when Hornclaw comes home
and politely wags her tail, she doesn't spring up or
rub against her. After a concise, dry greeting, perhaps
what she perceives to be the minimum requirement

of a cohabitant, she sniffs her, detecting gunpowder or chemicals or, most strongly, blood. Since chemicals don't smell sweet or otherwise delectable it wouldn't be all that strange for her to circle Hornclaw in confusion or bark, but Deadweight turns placidly away from her owner, impassive as always. Hornclaw often thinks that Deadweight's indifference makes them a perfect match. But she didn't name her accurately, as this dog knows when to approach and when to retreat, assessing her feelings and maintaining the appropriate distance—she would have been a more useful companion for someone else.

Hornclaw's ceremony of sorts begins by stroking Deadweight's head, placing her in her lap and turning eastward.

"Look. I left the window open."

Deadweight looks up, her gaze following Hornclaw's finger. The window by the sink opens to the outside, and the gap is large enough that the dog could wriggle out if need be. Once she brought Deadweight home, she called an interior designer and remodeled the window so that it would open at the slightest push; she never locks it. Before, she would open the window only for brief moments when she cleaned or to air out her space; she never otherwise kept windows open or unlocked. As a washed-up disease control specialist who is no longer a sought-after expert, she doesn't think anyone would break into her home at this point in her career, but she still checks the doors to make sure they're tightly sealed, a habit she developed working in the field.

Since getting Deadweight though, she leaves this window unlocked at all times. If it's cold or rainy she might close it temporarily, but she never locks it. At first she left a note on the fridge to remind herself to unlock the window every morning, but by now keeping it unlocked has become automatic, a reflex. She has shown Deadweight how to open the window many times, reminding her, "Don't you forget. You probably think I'm an old lady nagging you, but I'm telling you this because that day will come at some point."

Unmoved, Deadweight snuggles into her arms, not used to Hornclaw's embraces.

"If I don't come back, you go out through there. You see how it opens at the slightest touch, right? Don't slowly starve to death, waiting for an owner who won't return. You have to go out and survive, whether you look for someone who'll take care of you or dig through the trash. Make sure you don't get caught by a dogcatcher."

Deadweight looks up at her; it's not clear if she understands what Hornclaw is saying, but maybe she gets the gist from the rise and fall of her voice.

"Maybe this is easier to understand than the fact that I might not come back. Listen. If you wake up one morning and I'm lying down, not moving even when you nudge me and bark, that's also when you have to go out through the window. Not to find someone to help me. I'll be dead already. So that you live. And if you can't open that window you'll end up getting so hungry that you'll eventually eat me. I don't really mind if that helps you for a little bit, but it will start stinking and then there will be vermin coming through the pipes, and when people break in and see you, they'll have you put down. Partly because they'll think that a dog who ate its owner's corpse isn't in its right mind and can't live a normal life, and also because they'll worry that you could transmit germs or illness since you ate rotten flesh. But even more than that—you're so old that it'll be hard for you to find a new home."

Her speech finds its usual rhythm, and a peaceful stillness spreads through her as she rubs Deadweight's back. The dog nudges Hornclaw's chin with her damp nose.

"Not just because you're a dog. It's the same with people. They think that an old person can't live the rest of her life with her mind intact, that an old person gets sick easily and spreads disease, and that nobody will take care of the elderly. That's what they think about all living things. I haven't taken great care of you, but I still don't want to think about you being in that situation. That will make me feel unsettled, even when I'm dead. So when the time comes, get out of here and go where you need to go. Got it? Before you're considered worthless even though you're still alive."

She doesn't remember exactly when she brought the dog home, but she does know Deadweight couldn't have been the most adorable of dogs to begin with and that she must have brought her home since it was clear nobody would adopt her. What remains vivid is how she surprised herself, bringing home a living thing, an impulsive act entirely out of character.

She constantly prepares Deadweight for the future, but even though the possibility that Hornclaw will go out and never return is quite high, she continues to tell her *I'll be back.* She continues to say, *I'm home. How did you sleep? Go do your business in the bathroom. Here, eat. Drink up. Should we go for a walk? Don't bark, that's not someone suspicious. It's the gas company. It's a delivery person. They're delivering your food.* Until she brought her home, she didn't expect to once again have someone to greet, to hurry back to, a waiting companion. She didn't expect that she would again grow worried that she might never make it back home.

I'll be back.

Without turning to look at her, he told her not to say that.

She didn't have the courage to ask if he meant she shouldn't come back or that she shouldn't make a big deal out of something that was a given. Not coming back would mean she'd failed. Yet a good disease control specialist was supposed to approach every job as if they might not return. Hornclaw, however, needed to reassure herself that she'd successfully complete each job and come home—she had to keep saying it. Later she would wait until he wasn't looking and whisper, *I'll be back.* Somehow he'd still pick up on it and dismiss her without looking her way.

Her third act in life had begun in the shanties, when she was fifteen.

Her first had been in her parents' home. At twelve she left behind an older sister, three younger sisters, and a baby brother. In a cramped seven-pyeong house, her older sister looked after all the children as their mother earned money by threading beads and pasting envelopes. When the long-anticipated son was born, their father announced he would now make money honestly instead of by playing cards; he left home to find work, never to return. Instead of the eldest, who took care of the household, or the little ones, who were too small, she, the strong-enough, old-enough second-born with a good head on her shoulders, was the natural candidate to be adopted by their cousin and his wife, who were more economically comfortable. In reality, it was an adoption in name only; at the time, it was common for a family with many mouths to feed to lessen the burden by sending a child to a relative, and she knew very well that she was going there to be their live-in maid.

Her relatives weren't exactly friendly, but they at least didn't mistreat or abuse her, as was common, and though they did joke about her situation sometimes—where did her dad go, did he get himself killed or is he gallivanting around somewhere, avoiding responsibility—it wasn't out of malice, and they did try to be good people, at least in public.

Her cousin was the owner of some factory that made something of some sort, and his wife, who always wore a Western outfit instead of hanbok and held a beaded handbag wherever she went, smelled of fragrant face cream and Coty powder. They had a son and a daughter, and they were respectively three and five years older than her. She didn't quite know what to call them and so just used the generic honorifics Oppa and Eonni. Eonni kept her straight shoulder-length hair in pigtails, following the regulations of her renowned girls' high school, but when she came home from school she immediately put on a shiny silver ring, even though nobody outside the family would see it. Sometimes Eonni would pick out tarnished silver baubles from her jewelry box, her hands as soft as just-baked white bread in a storybook, and hand them to Hornclaw to polish. Timid-looking Oppa, who was in middle school, was taciturn and irritable, but he never forgot to thank her when she held out a tray of snacks at the designated time; he always left a piece of yanggaeng behind for her. She would savor the bean jelly slowly as she polished the tarnished silver jewelry with toothpaste. In this household, instead of salt or Number One powder, they used the Lucky brand that came out of a tube; amazed by squeezable toothpaste, she would oh-so-carefully squeeze a pea-size amount on the toothbrush so that she wouldn't waste any. Once the jewelry regained its luster after a hard scrub, she would try on a ring, which had fit Eonni's ring finger but was too big even for her own pointer. As she gazed at it under the bathroom lights she felt bliss—though that feeling may have come from the

scent of the fancy toothpaste and Coty soap rather than
the ring, which didn't have much significance to her.

One of each, a boy and a girl, a pair of infinite simplicity and rationality. As she observed their lives of
abundance, she would think of her own family's home
as a pigsty. It was so small that they had to sleep on
their sides, once almost suffocating the baby squashed
between them. It only occurred to her once she saw
how her relatives lived that her parents were like pigs,
mating, oinking, and having litter after litter, with
more hungry mouths than they could afford to feed.
It was unimaginable how her parents had found the
time and space to even do the deed in that tiny house
stuffed with sleeping children. She also couldn't think
of those old-fashioned ignoramuses as anything other
than pigs as they kept having baby after baby until they
finally had a boy, the family driving itself deeper and
deeper into poverty until they were all on the brink
of starvation and had to send the least clever or ugli-
est or hungriest child away.

Her relatives lived in a two-story Western-style
house with a piano, a telephone, even a television.
For her, they were marvels from an alien world; she
loved just observing them. The family also employed
a kitchen maid who was two years older than Oppa,

and she understood and accepted her assistant role with her entire being.

While the kitchen maid did the difficult work, like cooking, Hornclaw was sent to the market or washed the dishes with water left over from rinsing rice. Even though she went shopping every other day, the food basket, enough to feed six people, was always heavy; saving the water from the washed rice was also burdensome, and sometimes she used it all up scrubbing greasy dishes, causing the maid to scold her. The dish soap, which had been a gift from overseas by a client of the factory, was treasured as though it contained magical bubbles and used with discretion. Since the laundry was labor intensive, they did it together at first, but as Hornclaw got used to the work, she did all the clothes by herself, only getting help from the maid when washing large blankets. She also swept and mopped the entire house every day, watered and trimmed the shrubs in the garden that grew like clouds, and late at night she ironed her cousin's suit and Eonni's uniform for the following day; an entire day was not nearly enough to finish all of her chores.

Yet, listening to the sounds of Eonni playing the piano or hearing snatches of television, she felt she was living an elegant life. This family didn't scream at one another but conversed in low, considerate voices, and she vaguely understood that having plenty of food at all times was what made people's voices so quiet and gentle, as they never had to worry about their next meal.

She shared a room off the kitchen with the maid, large enough for both of them to lie on their backs and fling their limbs wide, but she tossed and turned in the strange vastness and ended up sleeping on her side against the wall, through which she sometimes heard her cousin and his wife talking. Sometimes they discussed her education, whether they needed to send her to school to learn to read and do simple arithmetic, and it seemed that they couldn't come to a conclusion between *why bother sending a girl to school* and *but she's family.*

She could have lived there without worrying about food or clothing, but she ended up leaving their house three days after she inadvertently flipped Oppa, the boy who looked like a consumptive poet from a bygone era, over her shoulder.

Around that time, Eonni was preparing to wed a bank executive's son, and wedding presents were being exchanged between the two families; the bride-to-be's bedroom looked like a storage unit as she went through her belongings, packed and threw things out. Her cousin had mentioned that once Eonni was married, she could take over the room and be allowed to go to school the following spring, the anticipation of which had put her in an excited mood. As she helped Eonni clean, the older girl sorted clothes that were too small or she didn't like anymore, putting each item of clothing up to Hornclaw to see how it looked, and Eonni's parents didn't stop her. She shied away, saying that this one might look nicer on the kitchen maid, but to be honest she was quietly proud of the fact that she was closer to family than the kitchen maid, and she also knew that whatever was too small for Eonni would also be too small for the maid. A room to herself, getting to go to school, a pile of new clothes and jewelry. Even though the room she shared with the kitchen maid was as big as a yard, her desires grew as her standard of living increased, and, sensing her rise in status as a relative of the family, she knew she deserved to be treated as such; even though she remained grateful that she had left the pigsty of her childhood, she suddenly realized that she wanted more.

That was the state she was in when she secretly snuck into Eonni's room after the dinner dishes, while the family watched television in the living room, to try on Eonni's ring and necklace, which were out on the vanity. She figured she could quickly try on the baubles and pose in the mirror—the bliss of it would set her ribs abuzz. But before she could truly revel in the moment, the kitchen maid shouted for her. Panicking and thinking only that she must leave immediately, she swept the jewelry not into their original boxes but into her own pocket, and it might have been a different story if she'd returned them later to their rightful places or at least handed them back to Eonni and apologized before the entire household erupted in turmoil the next day, but she became scared and hid them.

Her cousin and his wife searched the maids' room, unfolding each and every handkerchief kept in the smallest drawers, but the jewelry didn't turn up. The maid began to cry, upset at being a suspect, while Hornclaw herself pretended to be unfazed. The maid, who'd been thinking it unfair that the young girl's status had been rising but hadn't said anything so that she wouldn't be accused of unbecoming envy, insisted that she would take her pay and quit as soon as it was proven that she was innocent. Paying no attention to that, her cousin's wife searched both the kitchen maid's pockets and Hornclaw's, even inside their socks, but found nothing. Eonni demanded that they be stripped naked and searched again, but her refined mother scolded her. *Strip them naked? That's no way to treat people who've lived in the same house for years, eating the same food, like family. If they're not here, they're not here, and it's already more than enough that we suspected them this way.* She avoided Eonni's suspicious glare, feeling relief. Even if she'd been strip-searched it wouldn't have been easy to find the jewelry unless her cousin's wife was unusually sharp, as the ring and necklace in question were tucked inside her brassiere. A few months ago, the maid had given Hornclaw a hand-me-down, which looked like two handkerchiefs stitched together with straps, telling her this gift, which the older girl had received from the madam of the household, was from overseas and now too small. Until then she hadn't realized her body was changing. She'd quickly shoved the jewelry into the layers of fabric, ripping through the stitches; most people searched the body rather examining the clothes when strip-searching someone.

The next day, Eonni and her mother went out with the groom to buy a wardrobe for the newlyweds' household, and when Hornclaw returned home from the market she realized that the maid was out, too, at the bank. This was her chance.

She went to Eonni's room to put the jewelry back, but the door was locked. She spiraled with rage, forgetting that she had caused them to mistrust her. *Who do you people think you are?*

Right then, Oppa returned home and, grabbing her by the throat, he shook her, yelling that guilty thieves always come back to the scene of the crime. She dropped the jewelry. Oppa berated her, starting with her good-for-nothing father and her bad blood-line, using words like beggar and gambler and con artist and thief, and he accused her of hiding more things on her person and began to yank at her blouse. Next thing they knew, Oppa was flying through the air and his foot hit the hallway lamp hanging from the ceiling. Eonni and her mother appeared, having failed to meet up with the furniture maker, and discovered Oppa out cold, the light fixture having landed on his stomach. Only after seeing their shocked expressions did she realize what she'd done.

Oppa sustained a hairline fracture in his shoulder and his foot was put in a cast, and he had to stay in the hospital for a few extra days so that they could dig out the lamp shards and treat the infection. Their last act of kindness was to hand her ten thousand hwan, telling her it would be best to leave before Oppa came home.

It wasn't completely unexpected, but when she went back to her childhood home it seemed that nobody had been living there for at least six months. The neighbors had no clue where her family had gone;

for all they knew they had thrown themselves one by one into the river.

She sat listlessly in the empty house for some time, thinking she would have to return to her relatives and beg for forgiveness. She no longer had any pride left, so even though she knew exactly what awaited her if she were to return to that two-story house, she vowed she would endure it.

It was evening and the buses had stopped running for the day. She walked down the street, planning to knock on someone's door to ask if she could sleep there just for one night, when she found herself in a market lined with shanties and tents.

She had been clutching the ten thousand hwan tightly in the folds of her blouse, but her fear subsided now that she was in a bustling area. It seemed safer to be in a place like this, as long as she watched out for pickpockets. People were busily going about their own business, and even if someone gave her trouble, there were so many pedestrians about that she naively thought that someone would help, maybe even an American soldier. She still nurtured hope that there might be a spot of warmth in the world, despite having confronted its unkind true colors.

There were beauty parlors and clothing stores and general stores selling knives and hats and vests, with ration boxes stacked by the doorways; more common than those were bars, lit up with colorful spotlights, that blared foreign music. Instinctively she knew she should avoid those places, but she couldn't determine which way she should go, as everything looked the same wherever she turned.

A man came out of a nondescript general store hemmed in by bars, and he beckoned, maybe because it was obvious she was too young to be in this part of town. He looked half a dozen years older than Oppa. She was apprehensive about going into the store, but if anything were to happen she supposed she could do what she did to Oppa. Until then she had never even imagined that she'd possessed that kind of strength or skill. She must have grown strong from washing all the laundry and, startled, flung Oppa around without realizing what she was doing, and she wasn't entirely certain she could do it again. She let down her guard when she saw a woman—his wife?—poking her head out from behind him.

He was Ryu, the woman was Cho. In a small room in the corner of their store, she ate the meal Cho prepared for her.

She explained her situation, and Ryu asked if she would be interested in helping out in the kitchen of a nightclub. Even though she didn't really know what a nightclub was, she flinched, and caught Cho frowning. I'm not saying you should drink with the American soldiers and dance with them, Ryu said. Didn't you say you've done kitchen work before?

Her ears perked up at the familiar words: kitchen work. That seemed a hundred times better than throwing herself at her relatives' feet, begging for mercy, and now that her belly was full and her head was thinking rationally again, she couldn't be certain they would look kindly on her and welcome her back even if she prostrated herself, telling them that her family disappeared and appealing to their generosity. Now that someone was offering her work, the pride she'd believed had been snuffed out began to rear its head. *What am I, insane? Why would I ever go back?*

Wearing a huge, boxy T-shirt with English writing on it—maybe swear words, she had no idea—and cotton pants, both from Ryu's store, she hauled boxes of liquor bottles. The shoulder seam of the T-shirt went down to her elbows and the hem covered her knees like a sack. Even though she was small, she was strong and worked hard, so the manager of the nightclub didn't have any complaints about her other than her being underage.

One of the women she lived with by the back entrance of the nightclub told her it was polite to make

herself look decent for the guests and lent her face
powder, but she declined, saying she only went between the kitchen and the market anyway. Fine, her
roommate said, then turned toward the vanity and pat-
ted her own face with a thick, cushiony puff. Catch-
ing Hornclaw changing her clothes in the mirror, she
said, "There's another way to make money, but don't
let anyone convince you to do it no matter what the
manager says. I'm sure he won't try anything with
you since Ryu is the one who recommended you."

The manager of the nightclub was in his late forties and had a mischievous, smarmy side to him, often
touching her on the back or shoulder or behind for
no reason, but he didn't seem to be a bad person at
his core; she soon grew used to that kind of behavior. Having risen from being an unpaid live-in maid
to being compensated, however minimally, for her
labor, she was aware of the realities of life and knew
to accept unpleasant interactions as part of work, and
she sensed that because Ryu had vouched for her she
was receiving special treatment.

Still, as with any work that involved room and
board, the scope of the job often stretched beyond its
set boundaries, and as she carried liquor by the box,
heated up food, washed dishes and cleaned, she was
frequently called on to serve guests when it got bus-

ier and the music got louder. If she didn't have much hesitation around serving, it was because Ryu was generally at the bar, making her feel safe. Leaving the store to Cho, Ryu sat next to American soldiers who didn't have women sidled up to them, drinking beer for a while; perhaps he was expanding his mysterious network or devising a new business. He looked cool, conversing breezily in English with the soldiers, seemingly belonging to a different world than hers. When he spotted her he sometimes nodded in greeting; soon, that turned into a wave. If, embarrassed, she tried to pass by without acknowledging him, he would speak to her, the American soldiers' gazes swinging toward her as they pounded his shoulders or pointed, their body language asking *Who's this?*—all of which made her blush.

Late at night, she would recall Ryu's low voice and smiling eyes and put a hand on her swelling breasts, falling asleep to one of her roommates reading aloud in halting English. Flitting through dreams, she would see Cho, frowning, and the next morning she would feel numb and unwell.

That night it wasn't that busy; maybe the American soldiers were all on leave or something, and Ryu was drinking beer by himself at the bar, perhaps waiting for someone. Figuring that she could just work in the kitchen, she relaxed her tense shoulders and stretched. The manager came by and caressed her back, commenting, "You have a lot of free time, huh? Lucky you! I'm stuck dealing with higher taxes." So she straightened and picked up a perfectly clean plate and began to polish it for no reason.

It would have been a day like any other if the manager had brushed past like that, but she happened to look out the back door, through which he had walked out, and saw him standing outside, talking to an American soldier, his thumb pointing behind him to where she was, as the soldier craned to take a look. She was about to duck out of sight, but first decided to sit tight, wondering if she'd done something wrong. The looks from outside felt more and more pointed and overt as time went by. She shot a glance at Ryu, who was sitting within sight of the soldier, and mouthed, *"What are they saying out there*? He didn't answer, his mood irritable or maybe indifferent, and he turned his gaze away from her as he sipped his beer.

The manager let her off early so she said her goodbyes and retreated. She looked toward the bar, but Ryu was already gone. Maybe the person he was waiting for never showed up, or maybe they'd already had their meeting. She wanted to ask the manager what he had spoken about with the soldier outside, but it felt like she was making too big a deal about it; she knew there was a lot in the world she shouldn't stick her nose into. She slipped out the back door. The only thing that bothered her was how Ryu had avoided her, which was unlike him. While she sometimes pretended not to see him and turned away to focus on her work, today he'd ignored her despite her obvious signals. Along with Cho, Ryu was the subject of her eternal gratitude, and as there was nothing more to their relationship than the fact that she owed him for his kindness, his reactions should have no bearing on whether she was happy or sad. But, overlaid with Cho's disapproving expression from her dreams, his coolness toward her made her wonder if she had done something wrong. Maybe they had had a fight. Cho might have caught on to how she gazed at Ryu. *There's no way. I'm so busy these days and keep to myself and I don't even go over for meals that often. But maybe Ryu figured out how I feel and joked about it with her. And maybe that caused a misunderstanding and made them fight.*

Home was fewer than ten strides away. She started toward that direction when she felt the particular heat and shadow of a man behind her. Before she had the chance to look or react, a huge hand clamped over her mouth. The yeasty hand was so large that it nearly covered her entire face. Next, thick, strong arms wrapped around her waist, picked her up and carried her into a small shack in the opposite direction of home.

She didn't know whose place this was, but she understood her predicament as soon as she was thrown onto the cold linoleum floor in the dark room; the only way out was through the door they'd just entered, now blocked by the large man. He grabbed her arm as she tried to get away, but the room was so small that she ended up hitting her head against the wall. She let out a scream and held her head in her hands as the man, in a coaxing but threatening tone, said things she didn't understand. "Pipe down, easy, girl, I already paid for you." She stopped fighting for a moment, dazed by the incomprehensible English words coming at her. The man continued, letting out a sigh. "I gotta get my money's worth. It's a done deal. Okay?" All she understood was "money" and "okay," but that was more than enough to figure out what was going on.

Judging by his silhouette, the man would be able to squash Oppa with a finger, and the weight pressing down on her made it clear that she wouldn't be flipping him over her shoulder. Her ribs felt like they were about to splinter, and she started to lose her will to fight, but as her top was being torn off a face came to mind. She couldn't beat this huge man, but she did have the presence of mind to grab one of his fingers and bend it all the way back before he could tie her wrists above her head. For that he slapped her so hard that she thought her nose would slide off her face; he cursed at her and lifted his torso a little. For the brief moment he was distracted with his finger, she felt around the floor and grabbed something sharp. It felt like coarse metal, perhaps something that had fallen off a can or a hinge. It was longer than a toothpick but shorter than a chopstick, the size of a meat skewer. She instinctively slid it in her sleeve and steadied her breathing. The man bared his teeth and brought out a knife with which he sliced open the rest of her blouse; sensing that he would start slashing her flesh next, she quickly rolled over to her side. Her lower body was pinned so she couldn't get away fully, but she had been right; the knife landed where her head had been just moments ago and sliced off some of her hair. She wouldn't be able to escape his next move. He cursed again, pulling the knife out of the lino-leum, and she flicked her hand, yanked the skewer out of her sleeve, and shoved it straight into his face, a mere second before he was about to attack. It so hap-pened that she stabbed him through his open mouth; it must have pierced his throat as he didn't scream or say another word but, dropping his knife and clutching his neck, thudded to the side, his eyes rolling into the back of his head. He tried to pull the skewer out a few times, but it seemed to be hooked on muscle or bone, and in any case it was embedded deep enough that a person losing consciousness wouldn't be able to easily yank it out. But he wasn't dead yet—he was trembling, eyes wide open. If he managed to pull out the skewer, blood would splatter all over the room, including on her. Immobilized by pain and terror, the man couldn't do more than twitch, and if she called for help at this point and saved him somehow—though that didn't seem all that possible—could she insist that it was self-defense, or...

She could just run away.

He was a soldier from a nation protecting her country. Even if he didn't have jangling dog tags around his neck, all the foreigners who walked around this area were all here to do good, like this man, and no matter what she did she knew nobody would believe she had no other choice.

But Ryu.

Ryu, at least.

If she ran out right now and asked Ryu to help save this man, he wouldn't turn her away. His store was close by.

She had wanted to be in Ryu's good graces.

Even if their only connection was that he'd given her a chance.

Would it be better to flee and never see him again or risk his judgment?

She shook off the man's outstretched hand and moved to a corner of the room. She would wait for him to stop breathing. She couldn't have him survive after she ran away. The soldier gave up trying to grab her and instead attempted to drag himself along the ground to open the door, but he would have to pull it open, and even before pulling, he would have to lift himself up to unlatch the lock. With all of his remaining strength he heaved himself up and stretched his hand out to the lock. As soon as he unlatched it, she kicked him in the ribs, and the soldier crumpled like bearskin, dead eyed, and didn't move again.

The door swung open and she saw Ryu standing there.

All the blood rushed to her head. She'd nearly died a moment ago, yet this was more terrifying.

Without demanding how Ryu came to be here, what he'd heard and why he hadn't helped her, she began to plead. "I didn't mean to—he was the one— I—"

Ryu put a hand over her mouth and a finger to

his lips; he studied the man sprawled on the ground, skewered through the mouth, blood trickling out, and glanced around the room. "Not bad," he murmured.

She looked up at him, wondering if she'd misheard. He was smiling with what looked like genuine amazement. "I was about to beat him within an inch of his life," he said. "How much stuff do you have at your place?"

She shook her head frantically. She had a few clothes and she'd squirreled away some money from her wages under her pillow, which she'd been planning to give Cho. But otherwise she'd lived day to day, the simplicity of which revealed her desperate situation, and she didn't even have a single trinket, having vaguely imagined that anything worth treasuring would somehow involve Ryu and his family.

"Then go to the store," Ryu ordered. "Do what my wife tells you to do. Leave this to me. Go!" Ryu shoved her a little, and she ran, her thoughts scrambled, unable to figure out where coincidence began and Ryu's plan ended. With the conviction that if she started crying now she would crumple to the ground, she swallowed back her sobs. Her blood pumped throughout her body like a school of anchovies swimming in the ocean.

Only a month after leaving with Ryu and Cho,

who closed down their store, did she discover what Ryu's real job was. She would learn that the soldier she had skewered had been a threat. He'd smuggled goods out of the military base, sold them to night-clubs and stores, then tried to blackmail them. Though Ryu hadn't exactly been planning to put her through that ordeal, he wouldn't deny that he'd searched for a young girl—knowing what he knew about the sol-dier's preferences—to set up a honey trap. But his original plan had been merely to beat the guy up; she was the reason things ran afoul. She never asked how he disposed of the body and the evidence. Later, as she gained experience herself, the wonder and mys-tery would disappear as she grew accustomed to the process.

Hornclaw opens the front door, a long bag re-sembling a golf bag hanging from her shoulder, and Deadweight barks lightly. She looks back at her once more. The dog now sits quietly, watching Hornclaw, seemingly unwilling to stop her owner from doing something dangerous. A companion optimized to her owner's lifestyle.

Nowadays she has to say goodbye the moment she remembers to do it; otherwise, she'll instantly forget as soon as she turns away. She pets Deadweight on the head and says firmly, "I'll be back."

She'll be back as long as she is still breathing. As long as her hands and feet move; until the day this little pup is erased from her mind, until she can't recognize her anymore. She closes the door behind her.

When Hornclaw arrives at the office, a client in her midfifties is sitting across from Worryfixer with her arms and legs crossed. The client has brought an attaché case, splayed open on the coffee table between them; its innards, of course, are piles of fifty-thousand-won bills, and Worryfixer looks immensely tormented, as if they are suppressing the urge to grab the bills and throw them in the client's face. They nod to Hornclaw, but otherwise their attention is focused entirely on the client, who is decked out from head to toe.

"Director Sohn made me promises, which is why I'm here. This is unacceptable treatment. Are you going to do it or not?" Even though the client sounds entitled and annoyed, a trembling in her voice betrays her desperation.

Perhaps detecting that, or maybe because they suspect that the client has tried all the other agencies before arriving here, Worryfixer speaks firmly. "If Director Sohn promised you that we would take care of it, of course we will. But we need to take a closer look and conduct a thorough review before we give you a call. Especially because we haven't discussed it internally yet."

"Then I'll leave this with you. I expect a call today." The client puts her sunglasses on and stands up, her car keys jangling. Hornclaw is standing by the desk, and the client studies her as if she's appraising real estate.

Though the client is wearing sunglasses, Hornclaw senses that their eyes meet. The client cocks her head at this elderly woman, who doesn't seem like a client or a specialist but is for some reason loitering in the offices of a supposedly exclusive disease control agency. If a client looked at her that way just a decade ago, Hornclaw would have instantly drawn a knife and whirled it around as if it were an extension of her body, showing off her skills; she would have done that even if it wasn't her client. But as time passed her own reactions felt futile; she remembered how she used to be treated skeptically when she was younger, just because she was a woman. Now her age is just another reason for people to dismiss her on sight.

The client's heels clack down the stairs; Worryfixer closes the attaché case.

"The second worst thing in the world is people thinking money solves everything," Worryfixer grumbles. "The worst is people with unearned entitlement. That lady bursts in here and doesn't answer any questions, she just flips open the case, and she doesn't tell me until the very end that she talked to Director Sohn and he's agreed to it. She must think we owe it to her, that she's offering us a crazy amount of money. If she only knew the kind of people who come to us, and how much they pay!"

Hornclaw laughs. "She does seem a bit crass, but it's not the first time we've seen clients like that."

"You can tell instantly that she's a real estate speculator, right? All that jewelry she's wearing. No matter how much stuff she buys, none of it looks good on her."

"I guess Sohn's relationship with the powers that be isn't great these days. Where did he come across someone like that?"

"Who knows, maybe he met her at a bar. But if we're hired less often, you know it's not because of anything Director Sohn is doing. Times are changing… Everyone's smarter now and tracking things on social media. I'm sure some think that a traditional approach doesn't work anymore."

The prospective client's target for disease control is a twenty-nine-year-old man working as a host at a nightclub who supposedly preyed on her daughter for the past four years. Hearing that, Hornclaw wonders why it's necessary to get rid of someone so nonchalantly over something so minor; the client could hire any old task center, which could bury him up to his chin and extract tears and snot and piss before making him faint, after which he would gladly leave the daughter alone.

"Maybe the precious daughter is on a hunger strike or something," Hornclaw says. "These people think it's no big deal since someone else's hands are getting dirtied. I don't know how much money she brought, but just tell her to resolve family disputes within the bounds of the law. For us it wouldn't be a big deal since our hands are already dirty and it would be an easy job, but even I wouldn't do it, seeing that woman's bullshit."

"Of course it would be great if you handled it, Godmother, but that's not the whole story."

On the surface, it was about a daughter who had fallen so deeply for the host that she wouldn't leave him. But by the time her mother asked several task centers to handle the situation the daughter's drug addiction had progressed, and it turned out that the punk was a step above entry level, a director of some department or other, at a fairly large organized crime syndicate that was active in the entertainment and hospitality industries. His job as a host was just a cover. Based on that, three places had declined the job, all reluctant to get involved with that organization. If the client had kept networking and done more legwork, she might have found another agency that worked clandestinely with the organization in a tight checks-and-balances relationship, but before she could do that, her daughter fell into medication-induced shock while detoxing in the hospital and died. Having lost her only child, the client's singular goal in life became getting revenge on the man who first got her daughter hooked on drugs. After thrice making additional rounds she had come across Director Sohn, who boasted that he had connections with the organization in question.

Though she should refrain from asking any questions, Hornclaw suddenly remembers the woman's eyes behind her large, dark sunglasses, and imagines the resignation and urges that might be contained in those eyes, this client whose entitlement felt forced.

Then she laughs out loud, thinking about Sohn's

claims. What connections? What wouldn't he say to land a client, when he's done nothing himself and merely inherited the agency his father built?

"Tell Sohn this," Hornclaw says. "I don't know if I'm remembering correctly, but I'm pretty sure that a midlevel boss in the entertainment division owed Sohn's father a favor. Tell Sohn to notify him that they should look the other way when we collect what we're owed, it's just cutting off one leg. We'll take care of how to do it. Tell them it'll be hard to get their hands on their drugs for a while if they don't agree. We can block a couple of sources."

"I knew you would have some insight into this! Do you want to join him when he meets with them?"

Hornclaw looks at Worryfixer's relieved expression, and it's now obvious that they were going to ask her to find a way in.

"Look at me. No matter what I put on, it won't help, not with this face and this figure. The reason I was so trusted and well regarded once upon a time was because I didn't attend those meetings. Sometimes it's better not to meet face-to-face. Sohn can do that part on his own. He doesn't need me to wipe his ass every single time."

"Got it. But what made you change your mind about this case?"

Hornclaw doesn't answer, instead picking up the file the client left behind and waving it at Worry-fixer. "Call me when it's set. I'll have to get prepared. There's no way that…that *kid* would do something like this. Perfect for me."

Worryfixer looks puzzled for a moment at the sudden mention of the kid, then nods. "It's true. He's busy these days. He's on a long-term job, it's a month long."

"Did I ask for details?"

Hornclaw wonders if she should meet up with the client before going on the job, but decides against it. If she goes to discuss the job with the woman, who seemed unimpressed with Hornclaw during their brief encounter, the client's confidence in the agency is sure to nose-dive. Hornclaw knows that she no longer has the physique of a skilled disease control specialist. It won't be easy to disguise the age spots on her face, the sagging skin around her eyes and the deep shadows creasing her forehead, and the client would fail to hide her misgivings about how this stump of an old woman could possibly get rid of a young man in his prime. There is no need to worry the client that she might be wasting her money.

It's just that Hornclaw can't shake the premonition that the client will end her own life once the job is complete. She's witnessed from up close just how much damage a soul sustains when one's family is torn away, how that life withers like the skin peeled off an apple. Though it's just a feeling, she sensed from the client a deep sorrow—the aimlessness of a vine that has lost something to climb. Hornclaw has completed countless jobs over the last forty-five years, and though most of the targets had families, she never harbored any feelings for those left behind; there was no reason for it. For a brief period she was part of a strange family, slotted between Ryu and Cho, and then for some time it was just her and Ryu, but none of that made for an ordinary family. Even if she leaned on Ryu, even if Ryu had been her entire world, the feelings she had for him were a tangled knot of obsession and affection. If someone were to say that was because they weren't in a relationship, she could point to the child she'd carried for nine-and-a-half months, whom she'd handed over to an overseas adoption agency before the umbilical cord stump fell off, before she even stopped bleeding. A few nights later, her breasts full and aching, her hands had gripped the steering wheel as she drove to strangle someone.

She's never shared her life with anyone—though it's a bit inaccurate to call it a life as it's more about the mechanics of being alive—and she has never wished for a daily existence brimming with small joys and sorrows. When it grew weathered with time, she burned the newborn's picture in the stove; watching the image singe and crumple, not only did she not feel any regret, she felt a release. The occasional act of looking at the picture had been her way of experiencing the feelings a biological mother was obligated to feel—guilt, sadness and longing.

But now, she is noticing the emptiness in a stranger's eyes and feeling sympathy, an unexpected comprehension of what it's like to feel the tug of flesh and bone. What could this be if it isn't evidence of aging and decline?

The host in question is a middle manager with some authority, and since he lives in a town house he's clearly not at the very bottom of the organization. It's so early that the nightclub he operates in a tourist hotel is sunken in silence, and about a hundred yards away from the hotel is an unmarked building where the staff live. The town house is about a mile away; although it's not clear where the higher-ups live, she doesn't think they'd be among the rank and file.

Hornclaw keeps watch from a convenience store facing the town house, a paper cup of honey tea cooling in her hand. She's feeling uneasy because she hasn't figured out the host's daily routine yet even though it's her third day on the job. She wants to make her move before he goes to work so as to not leave any trace, but he hasn't shown himself. Maybe he's away on business? Supposedly he lives with his much younger siblings. At first, the midlevel boss came out strong, saying that they would handle the situation themselves according to internal policies. When Sohn emphasized how much he owed his late father, the midlevel boss finally approved the agency's plan, with the caveat that it shouldn't be done in front of the host's siblings. The midlevel boss told Sohn that nobody else at the organization knew what was about to happen and therefore no assistance would be given. At the office there were too many people who would defend the host, and the midlevel boss warned that if anything were to happen at the club there would be double payback. At home were those young siblings.

The only possible way for this to work is through a stakeout. As there is only a two-lane road between her and the town house, she keeps watch, changing her location frequently, but he doesn't show up; perhaps he was tipped off. Now, three days in, the client is beginning to call the agency, asking for updates. In the worst-case scenario, Hornclaw may have to disguise herself as a delivery person and finish the job in front of the siblings.

The part-time employee at the convenience store would surely glance at her quizzically if she stayed too long, a grandmother looking out of the plate glass window, killing time, having only purchased a single cup of honey tea. Nothing good can come from a questioning look.

She happens to look up and sees a man in his mid- to late-twenties emerging from the alley by the town house.

It's him.

Hornclaw leaves the convenience store with her paper cup of tea.

His hair is limp and unstyled, and he's wearing a jogging suit, but it's him. Still holding the cup in one hand, Hornclaw plays with the Buck knife in her pocket, slowly gaining ground. He crosses the street toward her. Oh, he must be out of cigarettes. She lets him brush past. He isn't dressed to go out, so he will probably go back home after his purchase. If at all possible she will do it in the confines of the town house complex, quickly, before he makes it to his place. Hornclaw downs the rest of her honey tea, crumples the cup and puts it in her pocket.

He emerges from the store with cigarettes and energy drinks in a clear plastic bag, and stumbles along as if he's hungover. Hornclaw follows at a distance. He

walks across the quiet two-lane road, barely checking for traffic, and just as Hornclaw is about to follow
him an old man with a cart piled high with recyclables pops out of nowhere and bumps into the target.
A pile of precariously stacked boxes brushes against
the target's shoulder, and he reflexively pushes them
away, snapping, "What the… "

The rubber tie securing the junk snaps and the
boxes and Styrofoam containers tumble off and scatter across the ground. The target turns his back and
walks away just as the entire cart topples over, and now
the junk hauler is pulling the tipped cart upright and
picking up his things while cars begin honking. The
mess occupies half the street as a man in a Peugeot rolls
down his window and swears; a Bentley screeches to
a stop, its driver visibly annoyed.

The old man must be used to receiving abuse, and
he calmly stacks the spilled junk back on his cart, unfazed by yelling or honking. As he picks his things
up they keep sliding off, and his slow movements
seem designed to stoke the drivers' anger; Hornclaw
quickly collects some of the boxes and moves them
to the sidewalk. There are so many that she'll have to
make multiple trips.

"Sir, just bring your cart over here. Quickly."

In defeat, the junk hauler pulls the cart to the side

of the road, and Hornclaw collects the rest of the mess. When the last sheet of newspaper is picked up, the cars rev and zoom terrifyingly close to Hornclaw, and the clogged two-lane road becomes quiet again.

"Oh, thank you so much," the old man says.

"You can take your time and put your things back on the cart here. If you block the cars like that…"

Of course people don't like it. That's what Hornclaw is about to say but she swallows it. The old man, who appears to have a limp, clearly isn't picking through trash as a hobby. She shakes her head, silently helping him stack the recyclables. The convenience store employee props the door open and gives them a pointed look, while pedestrians frown as they stomp over flattened boxes, one nearly trampling Hornclaw's hand. A person pushing a stroller with huge, tank-like tires chews gum loudly, waiting for them to clear the boxes from the sidewalk.

Only after the last box is removed does the stroller go by, jostling Hornclaw. Watching the baby's guardian, Hornclaw murmurs, "You could have gone by sooner if you helped."

"Oh, no," the old man says as he secures the recyclables with the severed cord now knotted together. "That's pretty polite, considering. Waiting without saying a word? You don't know the people in this neighborhood. I'm just grateful if they don't swear at me."

The cart still looks precarious, and Hornclaw worries that the stack will slide again before the man can get it to the junk shop.

"Thank you, ma'am."

"It looks like your cart is on its last legs. How much do you get for all this?"

"Are you interested in doing this work, too? You don't look like you'd need to."

"Oh… I don't want to be a burden to my son and his wife. Maybe I should pay for my own meals," says Hornclaw jokingly, then laughs.

"These days they don't pay much. For this—maybe it's fifty kilos—you'd probably get three thousand won. The going rate is about sixty or seventy won per kilo. If you can manage, it's probably better if you don't do it."

"Oh, don't worry, I'm not going to take over your territory. I don't even live here." Hornclaw helps the old man sling the cart handle around his waist and then claps him on the shoulder. "Look after yourself."

"Thank you. Have a nice day."

When he disappears from sight, Hornclaw's smile vanishes. She's lost sight of the target, she engaged in unnecessary conversation, she made herself visible to help a limping old man. She won't be able to come here tomorrow to keep watch, which means she'll have to change her approach. If she just ignored the old man, the job would have been done by now, but instead she's wasted the entire day. It's not too time-sensitive a matter, but still a failure according to her old exacting standards.

How, at this critical juncture, did she lose the target and instead help a stranger? If seeing the struggles of an ailing man close to her age drummed up feelings of compassion and sympathy, well, she's lived all this time perfectly well without those feelings and, in fact, managed to survive precisely because of her dulled instincts for them. But now it's becoming all too natural. Isn't that what an ordinary person would do, help a fallen person up and even gather their belongings?

Even though she knows she can still complete the job in the next few days, Hornclaw worries that her behavior of late is starting to resemble that of an average person. She clucks her tongue.

Tsk.

At that moment it feels as if the sound is coming not from inside her mouth but from outside her body; she flinches and looks around, but the convenience store employee has gone back inside, and nobody else is around. It has to be an auditory hallucination, as clear as if someone has spit directly into her ear, the sound carrying disgust and scorn. She quickens her steps; when she dashes into the narrow alley between buildings, she spots the edge of a gray coat vanishing around the corner. The scent of fougère lingers in the air as she cocks her head.

The kid? Why?

When eliminating this target, whose movements, as she confirms over several days, are confined to work and home, should she risk being recognized by the shopkeepers and neighbors, or risk entering his place of work, where two men always stand guard? After some consideration she selects the first option. If she were in better physical shape she would have chosen to head to his office and carry out the job that same day, but things are different nowadays.

Two days later, she returns to the neighborhood. Shopkeepers and workers from the Chinese restaurant are milling around outside, talking loudly. She's wearing a hat and a different outfit, and the worker in front of the convenience store isn't the clerk she saw two days ago, but when she notices the junk hauler's empty cart, her heart pounds.

She overhears the man from the convenience store telling a plainclothes detective that the old man single-

handedly collected all the recyclables in the neighborhood. He happened to spot him through the window,
and when he went to bring him some empty beverage
boxes, the old man collapsed; though he immediately
called the ambulance the old man was already dead
by the time the EMTs arrived.

"I'm telling you, I called as soon as I saw it happen.
I've only seen CPR done on TV. Am I supposed to
try it on him, when I don't even know what condi-
tion he's in? What if I broke his ribs? Anyway, why
are you asking me all this when they took him to the
hospital? As it is I was thinking of closing shop because business is so bad. Who's going to take over this
space now that something like this happened right in
front of the store?"

So he's the owner of the store. Hornclaw stays on
the outer edge of the crowd, but she can't bring herself
to look at the empty cart. She's seen so many people
die. Countless times, someone she saw the day before with a smile turned up dead the next day, most
sent off with her own hands. It's rare for her to discover that a stranger she randomly encountered is no
longer, his only legacy a large, shabby cart, though at
her age it wouldn't be strange for her to experience
something like this.

"Please. Don't take it out on us. We've been to the

hospital, and we understand what happened. But they say it might not be a simple heart attack. So that's why I'm asking if you've seen anyone suspicious around here."

"Anyone suspicious? I'm telling you, he was always trudging around by himself. Even when he fell he didn't bleed or anything so I just thought he was weak. If it's not a heart attack, are you saying he had some kind of wound? What are you talking about?"

Hornclaw knows how to make a heart stop without leaving behind any evidence. She could do that in her prime, long ago, but now she wouldn't even dare attempt it; it's not something just anyone can do, though if you strike the acupoints the right way it's certainly possible. Despite the convenience store owner's grumbling, the detective, perhaps because he can't reveal any more details about an investigation to a civilian or because it's just an idle conjecture on his part, says carelessly, "Thank you for your cooperation," and moves to leave.

The owner's finger stabs the air, pointing at the abandoned cart. "Come on! What are you going to do with this?"

"Someone will come and take it away. Please don't touch it. Just leave it here until then."

"So are you going to put tape all around the store because it's now an active police scene?"

"We would if it were a murder or a car crash, but since he was walking and fell on his own... I wouldn't worry too much about it."

After the detective leaves, someone reassures the crowd, saying there's no reason to be unsettled since it's just a spot where someone fell, and another grumbles that this incident will be bad for business for all the stores here. Someone else complains that the old man had to come all this way to cause so much trouble for them; finally, having vented to one another, they head back into their shops. Hornclaw feels dizzy, as if she's about to collapse. That a plainclothes cop is asking questions means that it wasn't a natural or accidental death. He was killed. By whom? The target. He was rude to the old man two days ago, but it makes no sense that he'd hunt him down and kill him. If he was that angry, he could have throttled the junk hauler right then.

Her footsteps quicken. She doesn't know where she should go, but anywhere is fine as long as she's alone. She feels herself beginning to hyperventilate, and she shoves her hands in her pockets, looking for the paper bag. If the police determine that this is a potential crime and return to speak with the convenience store employee from two days ago, he might remember an old woman speaking with the junk hauler, and then it would be just a matter of time before they scan CCTV footage. Of course, if she had succeeded in killing the target, the cameras would have caught only her back. But she knows that when she started speaking to the old man the cameras would have captured her face.

Everything swims before her eyes. She spots a basement pub and descends the stairs, but it's closed in the middle of the day. She slowly breathes into the paper bag.

She keeps breathing, thinking about Bullfight, who has a fourth-degree black belt in karate and probably knows other forms of martial arts as well. The fougère scent that lingered in the alley two days ago tickles the inside of her nose. Why? What is he trying to do? He's busy with his own jobs. There are other ways to interfere with an old lady near retirement. Why like this?

If the plan is to confuse her, it's worked remarkably well. It might be a joke to him, but she is immobilized by something more than irritation—she's stunned that he's suddenly getting in the way of her work. Everything feels murky now, like rice-washed water.

"Godmother, what's going on? Who could I reassign this to? Forget about the fact that you failed to reach the target. Don't you think there's a possibility that you're overreacting? It's so unlike you. You sound out of breath, like you saw something terrifying. Are you having a heart attack? You never mentioned you had heart problems… If it's dementia or something, just tell me. Tell me the truth. Did you go there with a spoon or a fork, not a knife? Even if you took a tea-spoon or a toothpick by mistake, I know that you'll use what you have and finish the job, no matter what the situation is. So what is this…? All right, fine. You did the legwork, they'll look the other way, I got it. I'll get someone else. Just go to the clinic. Don't go through the motions this time. I want a doctor's note about your physical state, whether you are able to continue working… Right, at this point I can't do anything about it. I can't keep it from Director Sohn. Don't worry, I'll make sure your payment is in your account as soon as you bring the doctor's note and sign an NDA. You're owed a lot so it won't be one payment, I'll have to do it quarterly… Oh, that's not something I can decide. Okay, I'll see you soon. I'm sorry to have to say this, but if you're going senile, you'll need someone to look after you, and you'll need money… So come on in before something happens that can't be fixed."

Worryfixer has never been the type to go overboard to flatter their elders and their frankness tended to verge on rudeness, but Hornclaw always looked the other way; she wasn't their mother. But this time, when Hornclaw calls to announce she can't finish the job, Worryfixer's tone turns noticeably frosty. They're probably more considerate when they have to dress down a first-timer who fails spectacularly at his first assignment and runs off, weeping. And here they are bluntly talking to Hornclaw about how she might be going senile or that the payments will come in on a quarterly basis. At first they seemed deeply disappointed that Hornclaw failed at the job, reacting with irritation, but as the conversation stretched on, it seemed they were convinced that it was finally time for this old, annoying hanger-on to be pushed out.

Hornclaw has nothing to say even when Worryfixer treats her this way; she doesn't have the mental capacity to be offended right now.

What is he trying to do?

She has told him she'd track him down and kill him if he got in her way, but that was just something she said offhand, not anticipating that he would actually interfere in her business. What's more chilling is whether or not she would have been able to complete her assignment even if he didn't mess things up by killing an innocent person. Now she wonders what

Bullfight really wants. It would be incredibly childish to do this just so that he can boast, "You underestimated me, Granny, but this is how good I am," and anyway it would have been more psychologically effective if he got to the target and did the job for her. Regardless, Bullfight would have nothing to gain. What would someone at the peak of his prowess get by feeling jubilation over an old woman like her?

But she isn't positive that it was Bullfight, and she doesn't want to get in touch with him just to ask him what he wants. It's not that she wants to avoid contact with him, it's more that she has the ominous feeling that she doesn't really want to know what's on his mind, what he might say. Plus, more immediately, what Hornclaw needs to do now is to get herself to the clinic as Worryfixer demanded, not because it's urgent, but because it would be more constructive to get a note from Dr. Chang stating that she's unable to do her job, instead of staying home in this state, mumbling to Deadweight, slowly losing her mind.

Her original plan was to say that she was having trouble gripping her knife, that the idea of approaching a target had grown terrifying, that there were times when she forgot a key detail and almost botched the job, that she didn't feel like herself at times; in other words, to exaggerate her current state in order to get as dramatic a note as possible. But now that she's sitting face-to-face with Dr. Kang, not Dr. Chang, Hornclaw has lost her will to embellish, and instead mentions a sniffle and a stomachache.

Dr. Kang, of course, instantly recognized her. *You saw nothing and nothing happened.* Even though he promised to look the other way, it would have been impossible not to remember the old woman who trashed the exam room with a broken IV bottle in the middle of the night or the sharp blades tucked away in her clothes. But he caught himself before his eyes widened. Hornclaw wondered for a moment if she could trust him and ask him to write a note after all, but she started off by saying that her throat hurts when she swallows. Those other symptoms, the ones she came prepared to share, are evidence of old age, and she doesn't want to confirm that she's sixty-five years old, at least to him.

When Hornclaw had checked in at the counter, Nurse Park said, "Dr. Chang isn't here today due to personal circumstances. Would you like to be seen by another doctor?" Although the nurse doesn't know this old woman's situation, she's worked here for five years and understands that she only sees Dr. Chang.

"That's unusual. Is everything all right?"

When Dr. Chang was at conferences the nurses mentioned his absence with pride and didn't hint at personal circumstances; Hornclaw detected confusion and agony in the nurse's phrasing.

Nurse Park looked over at the other patients sitting in the waiting room watching a drama on the HDTV on the wall, and lowered her voice. "He's not quite well."

Of course doctors were people, too, and could fall

sick, but that wasn't something that was usually revealed to patients.

"Must be more than being not quite well," Hornclaw murmured, wondering why else she would lower
her voice like that. Nurse Park, one of the nurses who
believed that this elderly woman was having an affair
with Dr. Chang, violated confidentiality by bringing
her fingers to her temple with a sad expression. Hornclaw understood that something had happened related
to the brain, and since Worryfixer hadn't said anything about it yesterday, it meant that Dr. Chang didn't
have an ongoing ailment but had been taken away
suddenly, without warning, and if that were the case
it could have been a stroke. It was clear he wouldn't
be able to return to work in the next few days; if she
went home now because Dr. Chang was incapaci-
tated, that would give the nurses even more to whisper about, so she finished checking in and sat down
to wait. Hornclaw's thoughts were careening, but the
traffic lights in her mind were still able to direct them.
One strand of thought involved her work and how
someone, possibly Bullfight, had interfered. Another
thought, tinged with sadness, went to Dr. Chang, and
that thought traced an arc to the old man with his cart;
it contained the sorrow that they were all heading toward extinction. The last thought she had was about

the fifty-fifty chance that she would face Dr. Kang today, since there were two internists on duty and she couldn't guess which doctor she would end up seeing; at that point, something resembling despair—or was it a sort of anticipation?—filled her lungs, and there was a high-pitched ringing in her ears.

The probability overtook her.

After listening to her heart and looking in her ears and her throat, Dr. Kang tilts his head. "You have a rapid heartbeat. Boom, boom, boom, like you just finished working out. We'll have to do an ECG to be more precise, but I don't suspect arrhythmia. I'm not hearing anything abnormal in your abdomen and your throat isn't swollen, either. But if your stomach is hurting and you have body aches and your pulse is this rapid, you might have a problem with your thyroid… Do you feel like you're sweating more or that you've lost weight? If you'd like a blood test, we'll get the results back in a few days, ma'am."

That's the one word she doesn't want to hear from him, but she doesn't argue, *I'm not ma'am.* "Oh, no. No need for that. It's so complicated to figure out one simple thing these days… I'm not that sweaty, I don't get that hot, and everything is the same, whether it's my weight or what I'm eating." Hornclaw waves away the suggestion, slightly panicking, making Dr. Kang laugh.

"No problem. You don't have to. Since you have body aches I'll prescribe some painkillers. If your stomach is more the problem, I'll give you a different medication. I won't add antibiotics since you're not running a fever. If the pain doesn't subside and you feel that your heart is jumping out of your chest, it would be a good idea to go to a big hospital. Would you like me to write you a referral? Or should we make do with an ECG?"

Hornclaw shakes her head. "It's all right. It could be psychological, so I'll just see how it goes."

"Okay. I don't think it's too serious at this point, either." Dr. Kang turns to the computer to enter the prescription and the nurse, who was standing with him, steps outside to call the next patient in.

"It'll just be a minute. You're all set."

"The peaches…" she says.

"I'm sorry?"

"The peaches. They're so good and sweet. From the market over there." She can't help herself; she wishes the words had a texture and a shape so that she could crumble them like cookies as they emerge from her mouth. What she just said could be received as a vague threat. She hasn't meant anything more than the fact that the fruit his parents sell is of high quality and taste wonderful, and that they also seem like good people, but in this context it could be understood in a different way. As if she's saying, *I know who your parents are and where to find them.* An abrupt reminder not to ever mention what happened that day to anyone, if he wants his parents to remain safe. If she were to bring up the girl's soft, cottony cheeks and the bean-shaped beauty mark by her pinkish ear, she would really be driving home the point.

But Dr. Kang either does not or pretends not to notice the malicious hints; he smiles and agrees with her. "Oh, have you stopped by my parents' store? They pick only the sweetest, freshest ones. I didn't even realize that fruit could be sour until I had it from somewhere else."

It's an overtly fake and exaggerated sentiment, but Hornclaw nods politely and smiles before regaining her edge.

"You should tell them you're my patient. They don't have discount coupons, but they'll probably give you a few extra."

"Oh, I couldn't do that. Not when they're trying to make a living." As she says that, Hornclaw realizes she's missed the opportunity to get up; more precisely, it dawns on her that she doesn't actually want to get up right away. And what she wants to listen to isn't a discussion about the sweetness of the fruit but his voice. Even if he'd misunderstood her intentions and spit out, *Don't you dare lay a hand on my parents*, she would have listened to his voice and held it tight. How could he remain so calm as he stitched the wounds of a shadowy person like her? Did he treat all his patients with the same consideration? Maybe he's only pretending to be calm, masking his terror, or maybe he is laughing it off, thinking, how dangerous could this tiny old lady be? As for the reason he still hasn't quit his job at this clinic? Is it because he can look the other way since he's just punching the clock? Or is it because he has to consider his daughter and parents, and the idea of moving from job to job like a migratory bird is too overwhelming?

She condenses all of these questions into one: "Don't you have something you want to say to me?"

She won't hurt his parents and daughter even if he doesn't plead with her, and if he wants her to stop she won't even go near the market. She asks this question not to hear what he will say but to hear his voice itself. This is finally when Dr. Kang's expression changes—he seems surprised that she's stopped pretending they're meeting for the first time today. The next patient opens the door and the nurse is standing there, too, so Hornclaw gets up.

"Oh, so…there is one thing," he says.

Hornclaw looks back.

The doctor looks confused and reluctant. "Please be sure not to take both prescriptions at the same time."

The old woman gets up from her spot beside her granddaughter, who is drawing a picture, and says, "It's been a while." This is only Hornclaw's second time here, and she can't tell if the other woman is a born shopkeeper with excellent memory, or if she's just saying that to be friendly. At one time in her life, Hornclaw never forgot a face. Even if she merely glimpsed someone, even if she only brushed past someone, the air movement or scent would act as a reminder the next time she saw that person. That was how she survived and how she did her work. But that talent gradually began to vanish, and it couldn't be only because her senses were dulling with age. Too many deaths had layered on top of one another, faces upon faces until nothing was left but black. Like the way the granddaughter has blackened over a color-ful page in her sketch pad and is preparing to scratch a drawing on it.

"You remember me?" Hornclaw asks.

"I don't remember exactly when you came in, but I do remember my husband hitting your bag... We have some nice tangerines today. Try some." The owner holds out a sample dish with a tangerine cut in half. It's small and has a thin peel.

"That's okay. I hate sour things."

"Oh, but this is so sweet, you might think it's honey."

"Then maybe I'll try it." Hornclaw takes the tangerine so as not to offend the owner. She peels it. Since it's soft she figures it won't be that sour, but it's even sweeter than she anticipated. The tangerine wedge crushes between her teeth, her tongue wraps around it, and a sweet coolness fills her mouth, elevating her serotonin levels. She gazes at the grandmother and her granddaughter; they are truly endearing. She likes to watch people whose lives aren't shrouded in darkness, who have put down roots under rays of the sun. If only she could own something of that life by gazing on it...if only she could dare enjoy the feeling of being part of a scene like that, just for a moment.

Even as she thinks it, she knows that her desire for that kind of happiness belies a yearning of sorts she has for Dr. Kang. Envying a family that is warm and soft like just-steamed rice cakes reminds her of her own position. Even if she weren't a disease control specialist but an average woman, her feelings would still be inappropriate, as she is so much older... Then again, if she hadn't been in this line of work, she wouldn't have met him.

"Her grandfather must be out on a delivery," Horn-claw says as she looks down at the girl, whose hand is stained purple, making it look like she has a bruise.

"Oh, there aren't a lot of deliveries these days. Business isn't so good. He actually went to a rally for small shop owners."

"I'm sure there are lots of protests against the big-box stores coming into the area."

"That's right. The authorities go on about how this is a protective zone for small businesses, but then of course they're in bed with big corporations, aren't they? My husband is the president of the small shop owners' association, so he's stuck in the middle. It's a tough position to be in. Powerful people call him in, and there are unspoken threats, too. On the surface they are conciliatory and say we'll take care of you, but the truth of the matter is—if you don't do what we say you're not going to like what happens."

"But surely you must not be as affected since all the big-box stores will be nearly a mile away?"

"Oh, but people will just drive over there now. They'll have parking lots and accept credit cards, and they'll also have indoor play areas for the kids. Once they open, I was thinking maybe we'd need to sell the shop, but then I think, who's going to take on a store like this that isn't doing so well? And he has responsibilities as the association president, so it won't be easy." The woman sighs.

Hornclaw doesn't know what she could do for Dr. Kang's mother—for this family—other than buying fruit, so she asks for a mesh bag of tangerines. Eight thousand won for a bag of ten isn't that cheap, but she opens her wallet anyway. A shadow drapes next to her. Her fingers, counting out the bills, pause. She feels a chill; anxious beads of sweat dot her temples as she forces her eyes nervously to the side. She sees Bullfight's profile; he's standing practically by her elbow, examining a hard persimmon.

"Do you have any soft persimmons?" Bullfight asks the owner, ignoring Hornclaw.

Hornclaw doesn't look him straight in the eye, but she can tell from his voice that he's smirking.

"We'll have those next week. But that one will kind of be like a soft persimmon if you leave it out for a few days."

"That's not the same. I'll have to come back."

As Bullfight pretends to mull it over, Hornclaw

pays for her fruit and takes the bag. She murmurs that she'll be back, turns around and walks out.

Don't run. Walk so that it doesn't look like I'm rushing, but fast enough that he can't follow me. But then she reconsiders—should I have stayed there? Did I leave that family vulnerable to him? Did he see the girl drawing in the store? Am I overthinking it, when he's probably just doing this to mess with me? But it is never overthinking it when it comes to the instincts of a disease control specialist, and it would be wiser to lure Bullfight away from the civilians. It's clear that he's here for her, since this isn't the usual territory for his jobs.

As these thoughts coil up inside her, she heads to exit the market, and someone grabs her by the shoulder. She spins instinctively, but stops herself from whirling the bag of fruit.

"Where are you running off to, Granny?" Bullfight notices her hand trembling and grins. "Want to do it here? In front of all these people?"

Hornclaw nods toward a shop closed for renovations, and they walk down the narrow alley right next to it.

She places the bag of fruit on an abandoned chair and breathes calmly. *If you feel that your heart is jumping out of your chest…* She recalls Dr. Kang's voice. That's exactly what it feels like, as if her heart is pounding outside her body. It sounds like all her muscles and nerves and organs, her guts, where the tangerine went not long ago, are exploding. She thinks of Dr. Kang's voice, flowing like a tranquil river, and her heart returns to a steady rhythm.

"Let me ask you point-blank. Did you get in my way?"

"Why don't you show me your hands first, Granny?" Bullfight opens both of his hands, indicating that he has no intention of fighting right by the market, even if nobody is around them now.

Hornclaw takes her hand out of her pocket; she was playing with her knife. "Did you get rid of that old man? An innocent person? Just to fuck me over?"

"Not to fuck you over, but yeah, I did."

"Okay, next question. Do you have bad eyesight?"

"Oh, this?" Bullfight takes off his oak-hued Swissflex glasses. "Nope. Twenty-twenty. This is just a disguise—"

Hornclaw's fist strikes Bullfight's left cheek, quickly, solidly, confidently. The blow is powerful enough to throw an ordinary person into the trash heap right behind him, but it just knocks Bullfight slightly off balance and makes him drop his glasses.

"Aren't you usually able to avoid being hit?"

"Granny, I'm just letting you get it out of your system. Feel better now?"

"No." Hornclaw watches as Bullfight bends down, picks up his glasses and dusts them off. "I wouldn't mind so much if that man was a witness or was involved in one of your jobs. But how many times have you sent off a civilian who has nothing to do with anything?"

Bullfight turns his head and spits out blood. "It's not the first time, that's for sure. And he did have something to do with something."

"Was he in the way of one of your jobs?"

"No. But you missed the timing on yours because of him." Bullfight watches happily as Hornclaw stands still, dazed by his words, her face turning a rage-filled red and then blue. "I don't approve," he continues. "In fact, I was irritated. Your judgment muddled by a heap of trash and a pushcart."

"Did you ever consider that maybe what troubled me wasn't the cart or the trash, but the person pulling it?"

"That's what I mean. Why were you helping someone right then? Human nature? Ethical duty? That's bullshit. Since when did you care about that stuff? Did you feel like you were looking at yourself getting old? How can you be so hypocritical? Think about how you've been living your life and the work you've been doing." His tone is indignant, but he still looks joyous somehow, like an excited child finding a long-forgotten toy in the attic. "Or maybe it occurred to you that you're the smallest, thinnest, raggediest piece of cardboard in that huge pile of garbage."

She clenches her teeth as each word jabs sharply at her joints. She's seen dead or dying people as often as she's had breakfast, and she refuses to feel guilty about an old junk hauler. She'll forget how her attempts to help brought about his demise. "I could have turned it around and completed the job within a few days. Doesn't it occur to you that you've completely blocked that option for me?"

Bullfight's sneer suggests that he doesn't believe she would have been able to complete the job regardless. "Okay, so blame me for your failure. It feels a little better if you have an excuse, right?"

Hornclaw fingers her knife again. The sensation of the knife handle begins to calm her down. She yanks open the plastic bag holding her purchase and tears through the mesh. "Have a tangerine."

A tangerine, right now?

She's playing up the grandmother role, reveling in how ridiculous it is, and she tosses a tangerine toward him. The fruit is as cold as sherbet.

Bullfight brings the tangerine to his swollen face. "Now can I ask you something?"

"Go right ahead."

"It's them, right? That shop owner and the little kid?"

Hornclaw drops the bag and a few of the tangerines spill out, rolling to a stop at the tip of Bullfight's shoes.

"I'm right. They're the ones. The people who made you this shameful. Actually, maybe it's not 'people.' Precisely speaking it's just one person you're distracted by."

Don't you have someone to show yourself off to?

He knows. Bullfight knows who I'm drawn to and what I want to hear, even better than I do. Suddenly Hornclaw can't breathe.

"You know how ridiculous you're being, right?" Bullfight continues.

She isn't sure if it's fear or shame that's enveloping her. "I don't know what you're talking about. Anyway, it's none of your business."

"Why wouldn't it be? Here you are, going around grinning like an idiot."

She meets Bullfight's angry gaze head-on. He must be only a few years younger than Dr. Kang. But it's not possible to look at him the same way as she does Dr. Kang. A newfound clarity washes over her.

"It's still my business," she manages. "I don't know what you're thinking but it's not the same as what happened with the junk hauler. If you touch even one hair on their heads, you're dead. I'll make sure of it." She is practically screaming. "What's your goal here? Why are you trying so hard to get under my skin? If you have a problem with me, deal with me. Don't drag random people into it."

"My goal? I don't know. What could my goal be?" Bullfight steps forward and eviscerates a tangerine with his foot, and the scent of burst fruit drenches the alley. "People always ask about other people's goals without knowing their own. Do you even know what you're doing right now? You don't even know where you're going, but you just keep moving forward."

Bullfight comes closer and Hornclaw grips her knife, just in case—if given the chance, she would cut off his flapping tongue.

"There's one thing I want you to understand," Bullfight continues. "The reason I said it's ridiculous isn't because he's thirty-six and you're sixty-five. How beautiful is that, loving someone you could have given birth to? Others might criticize you or point fingers, saying it's disgusting and you've lost your mind, but eventually it won't matter when you're both old. You have every right to look at him and think about him." He brushes past her, then bends down to whisper, "But you don't deserve to."

The sour tang of tangerines has covered the smell of fougère, but when she looks up, Bullfight is already gone.

As soon as she steps inside her apartment, Deadweight smells what's in the bag and follows close behind her. Hornclaw realizes she made a mistake. Since she lives with Deadweight as her only companion, she should have chosen something she could share with the dog. It won't be good to feed acidic fruit to a dog. Last time, when she came home with the peaches, she decided to check, just in case, and came across posts titled "Don't Feed Peaches to Pups," so she didn't. She vaguely remembers seeing something about grapes and tangerines on the list of what not to feed dogs.

The peaches. What did she do with them? She completely forgot about them. Even after handing one to the old man, she would have had three left; no, since Dr. Kang's mother gave her one extra, she should have four remaining. After she decided not to give any to Deadweight, she can't remember if she ate them, or when.

She opens the fridge. Since she lives alone and doesn't need to keep a lot of food, she has a midsize

model. When newlyweds choose appliances, they start
with the basic French door models, and anything as
small as hers would typically be used as a supplemen-
tal kimchi fridge. The bigger fridges get, the more
food gets wasted. When the 800-liter model came on
the market for the first time, she wondered what she
would use it for other than to briefly store a body that
was difficult to dispose of, and of course didn't buy it.
When frost covered the tops of the banchan containers in the back of the fridge, a repairman would suggest, *Ma'am, these parts are obsolete and it's about time to
get a new fridge,* but she always shook her head, saying,
*It still works, it's not like the freezer isn't working, and the
motor's not that loud, either.*

Parts are obsolete.

Broken. Obsolete.

It's time to get rid of it.

I'm telling you, it won't last much longer.

Replacement.

Hornclaw studies the inside of her fridge even
though it's sparse, with only kimchi and a few pack-
ets of banchan. Even that small amount has gone bad.
She might as well clean out the whole thing. She
opens the vegetable crisper.

And there they are, three brown, squished lumps
that used to be peaches, on the verge of complete

liquefaction. She must have eaten one when she got home and then put them out of her mind.

She opens a compost bag to throw away the once sweet, refreshing and ripe peaches. They should have filled someone's mouth at the peak of their flavor, but now they smell sour and putrid. When she picks one up, it falls apart immediately and dribbles. All because she used a little force to unstick it from the wall of the crisper. She has no choice but to fish out each crushed piece and slide it into the bag, then scratch with her fingernail at the bits stuck like cement against the wall. They have adhered firmly to the side, as if they have a lingering attachment to the frost overtaking the fridge. The sour stench burrows into her nose, making her eyes smart; a little later, her shoulders begin to shake and she lets out a moan as Deadweight comes over and barks gently, as if in consolation.

Two strands of white smoke undulated in the air and entwined together, resembling the arms of a mother embracing a child; Ryu looked up at it, at Cho and the baby combining into something intangible before dissipating, as Hornclaw stood by, watching him silently. Instead of grief or misery, Ryu's face held something resembling regret, the look of unfinished business. Hornclaw prayed first for forgiveness and then for their souls. *I'm sorry that I'm looking at him in his dark suit and white armband, at his shoulders, at his straight back and legs. I'm sorry for wanting to place my hand on his shoulders, for wanting to lean my cheek against his back—no, not because I want to do all that, but because I'm already imagining the sensation of doing so.*

It wasn't the first time she'd seen Ryu in formal wear, but he generally wore gray or navy suits, and even then it was when he had meetings with prominent, powerful clients. He had many different business cards with various business names, like such-and-such corporation, such-and-such industry, such-and-such food company, but his title was always director. Whether he was the director of a small family business or a shell company that kept switching signs, clients listened when he wore a suit and held out his business card. This was truly strange to Hornclaw, particularly because none of those clients really believed he was the head of whatever corporation. Rich and powerful people came to Ryu because they didn't want to dirty their hands, and those who were in a different social stratum came with all of their assets, in desperation, begging and groveling. Until he struck a deal with a middleman who handled imported goods and war supplies and got himself a business card for Disease Control with "Extermination of vermin and pests" below it, Ryu used the corporation and food company business cards in rotation, but people who came to him already knew what he did, what kinds of wishes he could grant them and what burdens he took care of.

Spellbound by the way he'd said, "Not bad," Hornclaw was by then handling half of his work. It was after she'd been taught all the clandestine skills Ryu had, four years after she'd first skewered the American soldier through the throat.

Cho wasn't a participant. She never even tried to participate. She was just an ordinary housewife. Taciturn and infinitely patient, she was a woman for whom it was a given she would have children, raise them, and not ask her man how and where he scraped the money together that helped her raise those children. She didn't try to know all the specifics of what Ryu did, but she knew enough to understand that his work was not merely unclean but also dangerous. She accepted that Hornclaw was helpful to him professionally and didn't complain about the length of time her husband and the girl he had rescued from the streets spent out of the house. Even when the girl grew up and was no longer a child Cho continued to make dinner for the two, even though they couldn't guarantee that they would return home in one piece on any given day. Hugely pregnant, doing their laundry, she must have looked down with a sliver of resentment at her husband's underwear and the girl's socks tangled in the water-filled basin. She maintained a strained smile, for the baby, but she couldn't always be above it all. Hornclaw could see the edges of Cho's smiling lips trembling with suppressed rage, so she forced herself not to look at Ryu. When she became skilled enough to carry out jobs alone, she asked for a place of her own.

"You've been such a big part of this, and I feel bad that I haven't been able to give you your cut in a timely way," Ryu began. "It won't be hard to get you a separate place somewhere. But how and where would a girl live on her own? If a girl your age lives alone, people will think you're loose, and it'll get harder for you to move around freely. In the end it's not good for the business. Are you that uncomfortable here with us, even with your own big room on the second floor? I guess you must be tired of hearing the baby crying day and night."

That's not it. It's you.

"I—feel—toward Madam—"

Ryu had told her to treat Cho as a sister since they were only five years apart, but she insisted on being formal, to build a breakwater around her heart to prevent it from trickling toward Ryu.

That's not why.

"Didn't I tell you not to be evasive and answer concisely?"

Hornclaw flinched at his strict, teacherly tone. She looked up and saw that Ryu had slid a cigarette between his lips. She picked up the matchbox and struck a light, hoping that her hand wouldn't shake too much. "I feel bad—that I'm such a burden."

She mashed all of her feelings together and euphemistically called it a burden; all the moments she spent with Ryu were branded on Hornclaw's head, hands, limbs, back, and neck. The smell of grass and gunpowder in the deserted forest as shots cracked, Ryu's touch as he stood behind her to correct her posture, saying, stand up straight, lift your arm higher, the tip of his shoe hitting her ankles as he told her, spread your legs wider, hold your head high. Her posture and demeanor were molded by Ryu's hands. Even though it never actually proved useful on the job—she always ended up hunched over or lying flat or hanging upside down—she was chiseled by him, indelibly.

And if something had to be done about it, it was this. A small, composed lie.

"Oh, is that all?" Ryu waved off her concerns. "It's not a burden to add an extra spoon to the dinner table. You don't make more work for anyone, and you bring in many more times the cost of keeping you fed, so don't worry about that."

No, Ryu, it was not the cost of food. How could he not know his own wife's feelings? Maybe he was pretending not to know. Hornclaw wanted to sigh.

"It's harder for me if you're not here," Ryu said. "So stop it."

Even though Hornclaw knew that he was referring to her usefulness as an employee, warmth pooled in the deep recesses of her heart. "I'm not saying I'm quitting."

"Same thing. Are you planning to commute? For this kind of work? That makes no sense. Don't make me regret teaching you all this."

"Don't worry, I'm not going to stab you in the back after your kindness. I'm not saying I'll set up my own company and steal clients. We can continue…"

"I'm not worried about that. I know you won't do something like that. Because you…"

What about me?

Hornclaw, worried that he knew how she felt about him, fiddled with the glass ashtray on the table.

"Never mind. But we're done talking about this." Ryu rubbed his cigarette out in irritation.

Cho, with the ten-month-old baby on her back, came in with a plate of fruit. Her movements were quiet, the ceramic plate not making a sound as it made contact with the glass tabletop, and her expression would have been calm and kind, but Hornclaw couldn't bring herself to raise her head and look at her; at the same time she was relieved that Cho had come in when Ryu's tone was so stern. *You saw it, you heard it, right? It's not my fault. Your husband doesn't want me to leave. Please don't look at me so silently like that, making me out to be the bad guy. I wouldn't articulate the dream I don't dare have...even if you weren't here.*

And then Cho and the baby were no longer here.

When Ryu and Hornclaw returned from a five-day business trip, they discovered Cho's body with her arms around the baby in Hornclaw's room on the second floor. She had been stabbed six times, in her back, her chest, her arms and her legs, and it appeared that the immediate cause of death was blunt force trauma to the back of her head. She must have been ambushed on the first floor by the front door, and instead of running toward the phone in the living room, she'd swept the baby into her arms. She wouldn't have been able to flee past the assailant and out the door, so instead, bleeding and holding the baby, she must have run up to Hornclaw's room and locked the door; since anti-burglary metal bars were installed on one side of the windows and a screen on the other, she likely attempted to rip down the screen to escape. When they came upon the scene, dull scissors from Hornclaw's pencil case were dangling from the half-cut screen. The door was broken down with

a hand ax or something similar before Cho could succeed, and she would have instinctively thrown herself
toward the baby, whom she had lain on the bed. And
knowing it was all over, she would have embraced the
baby with noble determination. The baby had been
strangled, an overreaction since they were in a remote
area and anyway nobody would be alarmed to hear a
crying baby; the attackers had placed the dead baby
next to Cho's body, and, perhaps as their last act of
courtesy, put her arms around the child before rigor
mortis set in.

"I—I told you."

Hornclaw hammered Ryu's shoulders with her fists.

"I told you we should forget it and hurry home."

Of course, even if they'd dropped what they were
doing and rushed back as soon as they felt something
was wrong, it would have taken them four hours by
car, and they wouldn't have been able to save mother
and child. They were on the second day of a job in the
countryside when Hornclaw said they should return
home. As he did every night when he was away from
his family, Ryu had called to hear the baby babble,
but Cho didn't pick up, and when he wondered what
was going on, Hornclaw grew worried. While Ryu
kept watch over the target's house, Hornclaw went
to the corner store on the edge of the neighborhood

and tried Cho again from the pay phone. She came
back, having failed to get through, and fretted out-
wardly, bringing up the possibility of carbon monox-
ide poisoning from the old fireplace or of a robbery.
If something bad were to happen to Cho, she felt it
would be because of her delusion that, somehow, im-
possibly, without a wife or a child, Ryu would lean
on her. And that meant she couldn't let anything happen to Cho. When Hornclaw first grew nervous, Ryu
brushed it off, saying it was often the case that Cho
couldn't pick up the phone if she was occupied with
the baby, or that she might have accidentally left the
phone off its cradle, and when Hornclaw attempted
to call every hour and failed to get through and insisted on going back, he chastised her for losing focus,
warning her that if she called home one more time
he would personally pull out all of her fingernails.
Maybe this was Ryu's attempt to suppress his own
anxiety. They were on a job concerning a not insig-
nificant political matter ordered by a powerful man,
and Hornclaw was fully aware that they couldn't stop
in the middle. If they quit or failed, they'd risk more
than money or their reputation—their safety would
no longer be guaranteed.

And because of that, her shouts turned into wails
and her fists pounded more forcefully against him.

Doing that made it possible for her to hide her secret desire, how she'd thought, *I wish something would happen to Cho*, even as she pretended all along to be a conscientious, considerate member of the family.

Ryu wasn't unaware that his business, which he had been gradually expanding, could one day swing back like a blade aimed at his family. He knew that the more blood he had on his hands and the more he successfully completed jobs, so the number of people and organizations targeting the family would grow. He had been considering various possibilities such as moving again or hiring someone to guard the house or telling his wife just enough about the dangers of his work to ensure that she would be put on alert without being too angry or afraid. This particular job was the largest and most important one he'd been hired for; this time he was mulling over sending his wife and child overseas for their safety afterward. Until he had a specific plan in place, he could only tell her, as if in passing, don't open the door for anyone, even if it's a person selling makeup or books, not even for the head of the neighborhood women's association or the police. No matter how he tried to puzzle through it, the only absolute way to keep them safe would be to never reveal to anyone that he had a family. That was what he should have done back when he ran the general store, but at the time Ryu hadn't thought everything through. He hadn't expected this work would dominate his life.

Even as requests were pouring in and business was booming, he still wasn't satisfied, and as the scope expanded and demands grew, he became more audacious. Treating his family as if they were in a crystal picture frame, invincible. Now his wife and child remained forever frozen in that frame.

After he went to sprinkle their ashes in the river, Ryu stayed out for a long time. When he came home he sank into the living room sofa and sat there in silence for hours. Hornclaw was watching over him from the other side of the room, thinking he'd fallen asleep, but suddenly his eyes opened a little and met hers, and then he grabbed the framed picture of Cho and the baby off the chest nearby and threw it. He was a little drunk, so his accuracy and speed were diminished, but before Hornclaw could lunge and catch it, it shattered by her feet, spraying shards of glass that scratched her cheek. This seemed to indicate she was indeed culpable for the tragedy.

It wouldn't be entirely wrong if that was how Ryu felt, Hornclaw thought, as she got off the sofa and crouched to pick up the glass.

"Leave it. You're going to hurt yourself." Ryu's voice was hoarse.

Hornclaw inadvertently let out a sigh-like laugh, then quickly clapped her hand over her mouth. How could she laugh at a time like this? Usually when she got a cut or broke a bone, it was because she was following Ryu's orders; sometimes he even caused the injuries. And now he was worried that she would get cut by shards of glass? Hornclaw picked up every last tiny piece; they sparkled under the lights as she poured them into an empty cardboard box. It was too difficult to pull the damaged picture out of the frame so she left it.

Watching Hornclaw sit down again, her back ramrod straight, Ryu smiled bitterly. "Don't sit there like that. Go get some rest."

Hearing how his voice cracked at the end of the sentence, Hornclaw instead went into the kitchen and brought him a cup of barley tea. She held out the cup; Ryu stared at it for a long time before he finally took it.

She looked down at her feet as he drained the cup. Her sense of guilt grew even more jagged at times like these, her heart stirring at the most trivial of movements, like the way he was now gulping down tea.

Her feelings deserved to be eviscerated without the possibility of ever sprouting up again.

"You're not listening to me. Will you understand if I tell you specifically that I want to be alone?"

"I know. I'm sorry, but that's the one thing that isn't possible."

"I'm not going to kill myself. Go to bed or do whatever you want."

"If you..."

If you go rest, I will, too. Hornclaw swallowed her words in the nick of time. On a day like this, she'd nearly told him to go rest in a room where there was no Cho, in the bed he used to share with her, next to the empty crib. But she couldn't suggest that he use her room on the second floor; the blood and the wreckage were cleaned up for the most part, but it was where Cho lost her life. She didn't know if she would ever be able to fall asleep with ease in that space herself, but it didn't matter since she didn't mind sleeping in the tiny room next to the kitchen. She couldn't rest while he was still out here.

"I'll stay where I want to," she said.

"Then I'll go."

He got up and went into the library; she couldn't bring herself to follow him all the way there. She stayed sitting, her knees pressed together, glaring at the now-empty spot on the sofa across from her.

Hornclaw flinched awake from some dream, and realized that, instead of the sofa, she was gazing at the patterned ivory wallpaper in the faint darkness. At some point, she had been moved to her room… but this was not her room. She was lying on her side, a blanket draped over her, and she felt the weight and warmth of someone's arm resting on her shoulder. She squirmed her finger out from under the blanket and discovered that it had been bandaged.

"Go back to sleep. It's only four." Ryu's low voice touched the back of her neck.

"If—" she murmured unconfidently, as if she were speaking to herself. "If you say we should quit, I will."

But even as she said that, Hornclaw was weighing the emptiness contained in those words. They both knew that they had already crossed the deep, wide river, and that the raft that could bring them back had already been destroyed. They'd come too far and nothing would bring back those who were gone; if they were to leave this line of work, people would retaliate. As long as they were acquainted with people in high places, they would have no other choice but to flee for the rest of their lives if they arbitrarily decided to sever those relationships, and anyway their lives were always at risk in this line of work. They were in an accelerating car and the only way they could stop was if they ran out of gas or flipped over. What awaited them was a cliff. In the short moment they were aloft in the air, their lives would be perfect. Then they would shatter against the boulders.

"I'll look into getting you a new ID and a plane ticket." His hoarse voice glided along her skin, his arm under her head.

She understood what he meant and quickly changed her tune. "No, that's not necessary. I've already come this far, so I'll just keep going."

If you're planning to send me away to die on your own, we might as well go all the way to the finish line together and end up in hell, side by side, since neither of us would be able to go where Cho and the baby are.

Perhaps that was their way of grieving. A kiss that happened naturally, two hands knitted together, over-whelmed by memory and despair and sorrow. They seemed to meld into one. If in that moment they'd silently decided not to die, it was for the other. Even though she was by Ryu's side in a manner she'd only dreamed of, Hornclaw couldn't actually believe she was with him. It was warm and gentle and loving, but those sensations were part of their mourning.

"Maybe we should hire a few more people," Ryu said.

"It'll be like a real company."

"I'll be president, you can be vice president."

"If I go up the ranks that quickly I might feel queasy."

"You can be president if I die first."

"If that happens—" Hornclaw paused.

"I'll install a figurehead," she said instead. "I'm not cut out to be the head of anything."

"If you want. But the most important thing is—"

Under the covers, they shared idle jokes, their toes squirming, more carefree than they'd ever been.

"You and me both, let's not make anything we have to protect," Ryu finished.

Hornclaw listened quietly, though it did occur to her that this wasn't quite the appropriate thing for him to say to her right now, as he held her tight. His embrace was a strange memorial service, signifying the first and last time they'd be together like this.

A breeze from the window made the mobile pieces hanging over the crib plink against each other, a sound like crying.

Let's not make anything we have to protect.

Ryu's words echo in Hornclaw's head when she looks down at the file Worryfixer hands her, at who is to be her last target.

As always, Worryfixer gathers the relevant documents. This would never be a possibility for any other specialist who is on their way out, but in consideration of their long partnership, Director Sohn has assigned her this final job, and requests that it be completed meticulously without any mistakes, as a proper finale to her career.

"Did you hear me, Godmother? Is there anything you don't understand?"

Hornclaw shakes her head begrudgingly. "I got it. But it makes me wonder—can I ask you who's ordering this hit? Doesn't look like it's anyone important."

"You're talking like we only go after important people! As always, I don't know the details."

"But if you don't know the details that would mean it's a pretty important job. The target's assets and his profession—he just doesn't seem like he'd have any relationship to anyone up high."

"You know that's not always the case."

Worryfixer is right. In this profession, someone becomes a target not because they have relationships to people in power, but because even a pebble grazing an important person's toe needs to be eliminated. Hornclaw taps the photocopied picture on the document, her tone casual, but it's the face of Dr. Kang's father. If it isn't because of a personal grudge, it has to be because he is the president of the small business association, which means there is someone working for the large corporation that has dominated the commercial area in the market. This makes it challenging. Even if she takes care of the person who requested this job, there would be someone else above that, popping up like a self-replicating cell, continuing to multiply until it becomes impossible to determine who ordered the hit. Even at her peak, she's never imagined striking the true mastermind of any job. She feels bad, but this man cannot be saved.

"If it's too difficult, should I find you another assignment? Something easier to understand, something simple, with dirty motives in plain sight?" Even as they speak caustically, Worryfixer doesn't hide their desperation; if Hornclaw doesn't take it who would they assign this to?

In the notes under the picture, there is a comment that seems to be the client's request: "As he's a merchant who interacts with customers frequently, please deploy an ordinary-looking, friendly senior citizen or a woman if possible." There are several people in their fifties and up who are still working, though they aren't very active, and there are quite a few women as well. But there is only one specialist who is old and also a woman.

"No, I'll do it. Don't give it to someone else. If you do I'm taking those earrings, with the ears too, of course." She points at Worryfixer's dangling half-carat diamond earrings.

Worryfixer covers both ears and steps back. "Stop it, you're being scary, Godmother. What did I do to be treated this way? You're too much. You're acting like this is someone you're having an affair with."

"No, but I've already sent off two men I've had affairs with. Once even with his baby in my belly. Want to hear more?"

"Please, no." Worryfixer avoids the older woman's gaze as if they're truly disgusted and goes into the office kitchenette.

Hornclaw folds Dr. Kang's father's face in half and puts it in her bag before leaving.

How can I send you off as painlessly as possible?
This is all Hornclaw thinks about. If she turns the assignment down, it will go to someone else, and that specialist isn't going to think about how to minimize the target's pain; this is why she took the job, but none of this actually changes anything.

The fee is ambiguous; it doesn't instantly illuminate the type of power that's behind this job. It's too meager to be a major corporation's attempt to disrupt small business owners and shove a big-box store into the neighborhood, but it's far too much for a personal grudge. The elder Kang is just the president of the small business association, not exactly a major threat to those in power. He held a press conference at the National Assembly demanding reform of the Distribution Industry Development Act, announcing that the small business owners would hold a rally in front of the building if their demands were not met, but that's something anyone in his role would do; he isn't a rabble-rouser. It doesn't seem that a man with chronic back pain who has a hard time riding a bicycle would suddenly turn his grievances into a battle.

Judging from the fee and file, Hornclaw gets the sense that the client's life would just become easier without the old man around; she doesn't detect the desperation of a client who would only be able to breathe again once the elder Kang were gone. Then again, quite a number of jobs ordered by important people are of this sort. They used to be even more common back in the day, when they sat face-to-face with whoever was hiring them, even if it was the client's most junior secretary, but now hits can be ordered via email or texted anonymously. It'd be nice if you could get rid of the maggots, but no big deal if you can't since there are other people lined up to do

this job—just don't think you can walk around with
your limbs intact, the client would say, sliding air-
plane tickets to China or Southeast Asia toward her.
After spending some time overseas at the conclusion
of the job, everyone back home had forgotten what
had happened.

She stops in her tracks and looks up. Without realizing it, she has started heading to the market. She
turns around. The old man who's loitering there sees
her here often, but it should be all right for him to
spot her again since he's not all there upstairs. She is
not planning anything at the market, and even if she
does and is noticed by that old man, she would be
quickly erased from his mind, focused as he is on the
past where all longing, love and resentments have already happened.

She's thinking about two wrenching things right
now. One is that Dr. Kang's father is probably going
to die, and the other is that this is the second time
in her life that she has wished to reduce the physical
pain of the target. The last time she felt this way, she
was dealing with the biological father of the child she
placed for adoption overseas, the father of the baby
whom she named whatever came to her mind and sent
away, worried that certain people would target and
eliminate the child. After that, from time to time she

had jobs targeting people she knew, but never again did she feel the same grief, regret and turmoil.

She imagines the arc of her knife as she stifles Kang's screams from behind and slices his throat. She will have to slash precisely so he doesn't have the chance to feel pain—no, since she is much shorter, that couldn't happen unless he's sitting down. Then maybe she has to slash his thighs—no, that won't fulfill her goal of making it as painless as possible. It will have to be the heart. That won't be easy. It's difficult to muster enough force to pierce the heart with a single blow, and she would have to put herself in a very dangerous situation. She's not as strong as before. She continues imagining what would happen next—Dr. Kang staring at her, looking devastated, eyes brimming with terror and disgust.

What would she say to him then?

Forget this.

She stops in her tracks; something glimmers, out of reach, in her memories.

She's said that before. When?

She hadn't been spotted at the scene much. When was the last time? She feels a sudden chill; the inside of her nose tickles.

"Excuse me, ma'am."

She looks up. It's the first time that the old man has

spoken to her. Even when she handed him a peach, he'd just stared at her, his eyes glittering.

"Are you talking to me?" she asks.

"Have you seen my wife? By the senior center here?"

Phew. Hornclaw lets out a sigh. "There isn't a senior center around here."

"Isn't this where K-dong Community Center is?"

"This is the market in S-dong. Are you lost? Do you need help contacting your family?" All she would do is call the patrol office, but she mentions the word "family," which people want to believe is a warmer, friendlier concept.

The old man snaps, "Why would I be lost? My house is right over there. But I don't know what happened to it. I don't see it. My wife went somewhere, I don't know."

Hornclaw figures his wife left this world a long time ago and avoids his gaze. "I see. Well, I haven't been to the senior center and I haven't seen your wife. Go on back home."

In this moment she sincerely believes that life might be easier if she forgot everything, like this old man, including how to return home, even though she's still sharp and sprightly. What would it be like to live a life that's trapped in an endlessly looping past until the day you die? What a sight it would be if she were in this man's shoes and all the acts that belong squarely in the past unfurled from her mouth like bundles of dried fish tied together. If she spoke of her past, the people around her—though it's doubtful there would be any people around her by that time—would get her admitted to a mental ward, saying she was senile or that she was going crazy. Though perhaps some would think she was speaking the truth, and not long afterward some disease control specialist would come by, disguised as a visitor or a medical professional, and probably add something to her medication.

Hornclaw wonders if her desire not to make the elder Kang suffer too much counts as protecting him as she turns toward the subway station.

As she departs, the old man murmurs, "Where did you go? You can't even move around easily by yourself. I have to help you. I have to keep you safe."

You and me both, let's not make anything we have to protect.

The person who said that left this world in the most ludicrous way.

Hornclaw was twenty-six, and instead of a shell company they had a real office with a proper sign hanging outside. They had two full-time employees, one in charge of answering phones and doing paperwork, and one who oversaw the warehouse, and both knew enough to understand that the company didn't exterminate rodents and insects, but did eliminate those who some might consider vermin. The warehouse worker, who maintained a continuous flow of supplies for before and after each job, eventually established his own business as a middleman for unregulated goods.

By this time Ryu rarely went out on jobs; Hornclaw handled most of them on her own. He accompanied her only when there was a meeting with a high-profile client or when making a new connection, and he instead focused on scouting new specialists and bringing them in. Hornclaw sometimes wanted to taunt him, asking him if he recruited people by doing the same thing he'd done to her long ago. The majority of the newbies were men, and most of them sported deep scars on their faces or tattoos on their arms, broadcasting the confidence that came with taking a life.

With more people joining and the business scaling up, they became a trusted resource for high-powered people. Each specialist's cut increased exponentially, but safety protocols diminished; even though Ryu was discerning with those he hired, every employee had their own desires and agendas, whether hidden or overt. By the time suspicious specialists were pushed out of the company, it was often too late, and since they had formidable talents and skills themselves, that move often brought trouble.

After losing Cho and the baby, Ryu and Horn-claw sold the remote Western-style house surrounded by fields and a creek and moved to the middle of the city, close to the Royal Hotel. Then they moved from house to house and office to office frequently while making sure the domestic moves and business moves didn't overlap. If they'd considered only safety, it would have been better to continue moving from inn to inn, but Ryu believed it was important to have a place to call home even when they didn't come home very often. It was strange for a man like Ryu, who'd lost his family in such a brutal way, to hold fast to this myth about home. The tangible elements of a home—furniture, clothes, kitchen appliances—all became baggage; in fact, baggage was the most important factor in creating a home. There was no way to bring all those burdens with you if you went from place to place, and while Hornclaw, who was used to fleeing with only the clothes on her back, considered home unimportant, a place to put leftover rice cakes or half-chewed gum, Ryu insisted on having one. Yet he disliked hearing her say she'd be back, and he still acted as though there was no tomorrow.

Then again, the threats against their home and office weren't so frequent that they had to be prepared
to leave at any moment. Right when they were about
to forget about the last incident, a homemade bomb or
a bag containing a flayed animal corpse would arrive
like a note from an obsessed ex-lover. Some were sent
by the powerful to threaten them, but as the company's influence grew, their former staff would sometimes band together and attack. When he couldn't
look the other way anymore, Ryu would gather his
specialists and engage in an extensive cleanup.

Even though Ryu didn't go on the jobs, he was
often away, nurturing relationships with the powerful,
so a housekeeper in her fifties was usually the only one
at home. She was a proven loyalist, who had answered
phones in the office for two years before retiring due
to chronic laryngitis unrelated to the job, then came
to work for them at home, moving with them every
time. She kept house, cooked and cleaned, and she was
so frugal that she could send extra savings to her son
and his wife. Her bosses were gone all day long, so
she would often take breaks to lie on the sofa, watch
television and nap; she worked with great satisfaction,
since there was nobody badgering her and her budget for household expenses was generous. Whenever
Hornclaw stepped through the front door late at night

and smelled mackerel broiling or heard zucchini bubbling in the soup and spotted the housekeeper working in the kitchen, she felt safe; that must have been the function and mythology of the concept of home Ryu believed in.

But then, one night, Ryu and Hornclaw returned after a meeting with a powerful person's junior deputy. It was very late. She usually shied away from those types of meetings, but the deputy had wanted to meet her; she joined them, without having changed into something more appropriate, without having had the chance to completely scrub off the smell of blood. She refilled empty liquor cups and the deputy sent away the gisaeng to have Hornclaw do all the various tasks. He had her sit next to him, commented on her appearance, needled her about not wearing a nice skirt, kept touching her hair and face, and held her wrist tightly, asking how she could possibly do the work with such thin wrists. While Ryu turned a little pale, he didn't intervene, which annoyed her. *You always do what you want and never think about how I might feel. You always tell me to forget about feelings.*

It was meaningless to grumble; if she did, Ryu would snort and tell her that she was supposed to protect herself. If she were to ask with her eyes if she could kill this asshole, he'd answer silently back that she should do whatever the deputy asked.

As they approached home, Ryu ran after her and tried to put a hand on her shoulder, which she shook off. She looked up and saw that all the windows were dark. Thinking that the housekeeper must be asleep since it was so late, Hornclaw slid her key in the door.

When she pushed the door open, she didn't feel any warmth from inside. Though their housekeeper scrimped on coal briquettes and didn't keep the house well heated throughout the day, she always had it warm at night when her bosses could return at any moment; she even woke up in the middle of the night to change out the briquettes, and it was now long past when new briquettes would have been added. Hornclaw instantly realized that there was some sort of trouble at home. She closed the door and took out her Colt .45 from her holster. Ryu, standing behind her, was ready. They glanced at each other, then nodded.

Hornclaw kicked the door open and slid in on one knee. They heard only their guns cocking as they aimed to the left and the right; there was no reaction from inside. Ryu looked around and turned on the living room lights, and that was when they saw the housekeeper's arm dangling behind the sofa. Hornclaw went over and saw that the housekeeper's face was peaceful and her eyes were closed; though Hornclaw didn't immediately see any wounds, blood from the back of the housekeeper's head had pooled on the leather sofa.

Right then, something fell from its perch above the front door and rolled on the floor all the way under the sofa. A ticking noise came from below, having been jolted to life by the impact. Before either of them could utter, "Get away!" it exploded.

Hornclaw opened her eyes and crawled out from under Ryu, who was heavy over her shoulders and head. The hardwood floor had cratered; the sofa and the housekeeper's body had been flung up, cushioning the blow, but the lower half of Ryu's body had flown and scattered. One of his ankles rolled in front of the broken living room window.

Ryu's eyelids twitched. Blood was soaking one cheek, so she couldn't see clearly what his blinking was trying to convey.

"Director…"

Didn't you always say that you have to protect yourself? Hornclaw couldn't say anything through her gritted teeth. She couldn't let tears cloud her vision. She had to witness his final moments; she had to listen carefully for a possible message. A huge convulsion overtook what remained of his body. It seemed like a faint smile of relief flashed across his face before his head fell limply in her lap.

Afterward, though it wasn't quite right to call it her last gift to Ryu, she moved manically, skillfully handling the problems that had piled up. First she sorted the various files by year; though she was planning to incinerate the entire lot, she wanted to check that there wasn't any omitted document before she did so. She laid off the full-time employees, notified freelancers that she was canceling their contracts and went to meet the middleman for unregulated goods, the officials at the pharmaceutical company, pharmacists and chemists. When she met with the deputies of large corporations, they lamented that they couldn't trust anyone else and begged her to return to work; sometimes even politicians joined in their entreaties. She emphasized the fact that she was uneducated, that she only knew how to be the muscle, and that nothing could be done without Ryu, thinking all the while that one of these friendly, smiling people could have ordered Ryu's death. And that a knife could land in her back as soon as she turned around.

But what stabbed her in the back when she stood and turned to go after one particular meeting was a cabinet minister's comment. "You must have divine luck to be able to survive that."

Ryu blocked it, not God. Shoving the retort back down her throat, Hornclaw grabbed the handle of the sliding door.

"Don't you think it's because it's your destiny to continue? Listen. An organization doesn't vanish because the chief suddenly gets tired and tells his staff, 'we're disbanding as of today.' The organization is already running, all the parts working in concert. Until all the components are gone it will keep functioning. If you don't want to be the head of the organization, I would hope you'd continue as the arms and legs. I can find someone who's smart and trustworthy and have him be the chief. Aren't you too young to give it all up?"

She finally accepted that proposal a few months later. She'd experienced a series of minor incidents, like a flowerpot falling from above as she walked by, but that wasn't why she decided to continue in this line of work. She had thought about whether Ryu would want her to follow him into the afterlife immediately or live out her life, before coming to the conclusion that Ryu wouldn't want anything from her either way. She never thought about fulfilling Ryu's dying wishes, not that he would have had dying wishes to begin with. Her life was halted in the present. She grabbed her tools because she didn't have any expectations or hopes for the future, because she was alive, because she opened her eyes that morning. She didn't think about the reason she existed, she didn't form justifications for her behavior or give meaning to it. She didn't try too hard to survive and she didn't try too hard to die before her time. Moving only because her heart was still beating was the attribute of a superior machine. She thought of Ryu occasionally and remembered his teachings, but beyond the sensation of the calluses on her palms caused by the tools that were an extension of her body, she no longer ached or longed for him. She was getting older.

The elder Kang presses the kindergarten doorbell at four in the afternoon, like he always does. The bell feels loose, like it's broken; no matter how many times he presses, he doesn't hear anything, so he pulls the door, which opens gently. He approaches the teachers' office on the first floor and knocks, and Haeni's teacher comes out to greet him.

"Hello, I'm here to pick Haeni up. You should really put a sign on the door that the bell's broken…"

The teacher tilts her head. "It's broken? Didn't it ring?"

"Well, our bell at home is so old that when it's cold it crackles all winter long and sometimes it doesn't work. And the door was open, too?"

"Oh, really? It's an automatic lock with an antitheft system, so that's odd…"

The old man doesn't understand the fancy words coming out of the teacher's mouth, so he clears his throat and changes the subject. "Anyway, you should call someone to fix it. Is Haeni ready?"

"The door locks automatically, so you can't open it from the outside without taking it off the hinges. Anyway, let me put in a call for Haeni." The teacher goes into the office to make the call, then dashes out, her face pale. "There's a problem. Haeni's not here."

Kang blinks, unable to understand what's going on.

"Her bag and jacket are still here, but it's been a while since she went to the bathroom, and now nobody can find her, she's not there…"

Blood rushes to Kang's head as his heart begins to pound. An amorphous, textured fear starts to gather.

The store is shuttered and padlocked without even a hastily scribbled sign saying it's closed today. Horn-claw goes over what she was planning to do by coming here. Right now, she really should be avoiding the target, not visiting him. Did she come here to buy fruit? Or was she planning to confess everything, warn him to close the store and stay home for a while? Though nothing will be solved by his closing the store. What if she tells him, just hand the small business association position to someone else, anyone, and stay in hiding? No matter how urgent her warning, it's going to come off as nonsense unless she reveals her true identity. And it's unlikely that the client will readily cross the target's name off the list just because the elder Kang's professional status has changed. There's nothing she can do.

Still, it concerns her that the store is closed; maybe the wife, who looked unwell, ended up taking to her sickbed. Or maybe his back pain got so bad that he is no longer able to make deliveries. They would be stretched too thin for the wife to stay home and hire a young part-timer. The woman told Hornclaw nobody came to the market to buy fruit anymore. Hornclaw had thought that the market would still draw people for vegetables and fruit, if not for industrial products. Regardless of labor costs, they really did need someone stronger to work at the store; the woman looked too frail to pick up a watermelon.

Right then, someone yanks Hornclaw by the nape of her neck, and she reflexively snaps her head back, strikes the person under the nose, digs her elbow into his sternum, spins around and shoves him against the shutters, her hand gripping the front of his shirt. When she finally takes a careful look, it's Dr. Kang. He's not wearing his doctor's coat. Why is he at his parents' store at this hour?

"Got—you," he croaks, even though he's the one immobilized and subdued, and Hornclaw nearly laughs, but she notices his gaunt, unshaven face and his uneven voice. "It's because of you, isn't it? Why it happened to us? I knew you'd come by at some point so I was watching from over there."

"What...?" She lets go and Dr. Kang slides down, coughing, then hawks and spits, his clothes still disheveled; perhaps she injured his teeth, as blood is mixed in with his spit as it bubbles on the ground.

She slips her hand into her coat pocket, feeling foolish. "It looks like your mouth is bleeding. Maybe you should get it checked out? I'm sorry about this. You shouldn't surprise someone like that. What's going on? Why are you here and not at the clinic?"

"It's all because of you! What did you do?"

There's no rule that someone has to act the same whether or not he's wearing a doctor's coat, but she's never pictured him this way. His tone is sharp and rough, and he is shaking with hatred and disgust.

Hornclaw suddenly feels guilty, wondering if he somehow knows about her plan, but she tries to maintain her calm. She hasn't actually done anything yet.

"What do you mean?" she asks. "I just came to buy some fruit, and I wondered if something happened since the store's closed."

Dr. Kang yanks out a piece of paper, folded twice, and throws it at her. The stiff paper whirls toward her and hits her on the nose as she stands there, confused. "How can you pretend to know nothing?"

She tries not to notice how her fingers are trembling as she unfolds the paper.

Dr. Kang gets up from the ground. "She's gone."

And he finally bursts into tears.

The girl's father took emergency leave from the clinic and held his elderly parents by the hand. He reassured them it was not their fault. He couldn't begin to guess why his child disappeared. He'd already called his late wife's side of the family—a small unit composed of the girl's grandmother and unmarried aunt—from whom they have been distant for a few years. They were welcome to see the girl anytime they wanted, but they kept their distance after his wife's death, to deal with their own grief. Still their relationship with Dr. Kang has always been good—two years ago, during Chuseok, they'd even made an effort to meet up. And anyway, if that side of the family took Haeni, they would have confidently walked into the school and asked for the child instead of tampering with the lock.

Though it hadn't yet been twenty-four hours, the police sent investigators to the grandparents' home, since the missing person was a six-year-old. A few of them smoked in the yard, rubbing their cigarettes out in the planters, and talked about how, back in the day, there was no way they would be assigned to a case until after twenty-four hours had passed, and shared other stories from the Bronze Age. But the likelihood of a kidnapped child being found alive is highest during the first seventy-two hours. These days, even if it turned out that they wasted investigative resources for a missing child who turns out to be a runaway, they had to immediately start working on it since there is so much online commentary.

The investigators reviewed CCTV footage in the neighborhood and caught a glimpse of a woman walking with a young girl not wearing a coat. The image was fuzzy, spotted and distorted, and the grandmother was in such a state of shock that even when she was asked if the girl in the footage was her granddaughter, she just blinked unconfidently, which was understandable. The screen was so small and the subjects were so far away that the image turned pixelated when they zoomed in. The grandmother couldn't remember what her granddaughter was wearing that morning, and the father wasn't the one who dressed her. In any case, there was no other explanation as the time stamp on the video matched the window of the girl's disappearance, and though the investigators asked the family if they knew this woman, they couldn't tell who it was no matter how closely they looked, and it wasn't even entirely clear if it was a woman.

The police asked if the family had enrolled the girl's fingerprints in the national registry as a precautionary measure in case she was kidnapped or got lost. Dr. Kang and his parents didn't know what they were talking about. The police figured that young parents these days automatically enrolled for the service, so one of the investigators looked it up but found no data. The investigator looked up at the child's father in exasperation. You didn't enroll her? Doctor, are you a Red or something? The type that talks about how they oppose the government collecting and maintaining a fingerprint registry? Dr. Kang was incensed by the accusation but didn't have the energy to grab the officer by the throat; and anyway since he was the one asking for police assistance to find his daughter, the investigators had all the power and he had to do what he was told. In all honesty, Dr. Kang wasn't organized enough to open Haeni's backpack every day after school and read the kindergarten newsletter sent home every Friday. After the death of his wife, he thought he should fulfill a mother's role for his daughter, but he didn't have the right personality for it. He tended to rely on his own aging mother to take care of things. Certainly the kindergarten would have sent home a notice about enrollment along with the application, but Dr. Kang never saw it. His mother would have kept it to discuss with her son later, not knowing what it all meant, then pushing it to another day and then another, since there were precious few hours in a day and they were all so busy with work.

The father and grandfather were silent and the grandmother lay on the sofa across from them, blinking in and out of consciousness. The police hooked up their home phone to recording and tracing equipment, but no call demanding money came. It occurred to Dr. Kang that if someone were to call for ransom—though who would demand money from a family consisting of a contract doctor and fruit sellers who were about to lose their business?—it might go to his cell phone, and told the investigators that he'd go back to the clinic for it. Since he knew that parents were the first suspects when a child went missing, whether because of domestic abuse or mental illness, he assumed that an officer would accompany him, but as they were short-staffed they chose to confirm that he spent all day in the clinic examining patients the previous day and allowed him to go on his own.

When he arrived at the clinic, a downcast nurse handed him a fax, saying it had just come for him. Dr. Kang read it, then stood dazed for a while, before intuiting that this was related to that strange old woman. Based on her demeanor and actions, he determined that he needed to see her before giving the fax to the police.

"But then it turns out the phone number in your file is fake, and even your name is fake. Since you're clearly after something, I thought you'd come by here. So what do you want from us? Why is this happening to us? Where is my Haeni!"

Hornclaw is putting together the pieces of the situation one by one, and doesn't fully hear Dr. Kang's wail.

She's eating and sleeping well. I bought her a warm new coat, too. She didn't eat any fruit, maybe because her family owns a fruit stand. But she did have two bowls of vanilla ice cream, even though it's so cold out. Don't worry, she didn't get a stomachache. For dinner she had chard soup and broiled cutlassfish, and for breakfast she had young radish kimchi and a fried egg. She's all grown up, brushing her own teeth when given a new toothbrush. I hope this helps you feel a little relieved. If you'd like to see her again, please tell that old granny to come by herself to the following address at 2 p.m. on the 5th. Remember, on the 5th. Even if you go straight to the police now, there's nothing at the address, and you'll just be putting her in danger. If there's anyone other than that granny who comes on the 5th, you won't see the girl alive.

This is followed by the address. The tone of the letter is polite and cold, and somehow mocking.

"I don't think it's referring to anyone else, this granny in the letter. They certainly don't mean Haeni's grandma. This is so frustrating. Please, say something. What did we do to you? I didn't talk, I stayed quiet like you told me to, and I told you from the beginning that I don't care what it is you do. So why are you toying with an innocent person? What exactly do you want?"

"Shut up, will you?" Hornclaw bellows, still staring at the fax. Her neural circuits are misfiring and connecting to the wrong places until finally she realizes that the sender of the fax is Bullfight. He's calling her. He would have used a fake name to request the hit on the elder Kang, and that would have been a ploy to distract her. Because Bullfight is targeting this entire family, and using them to get to her.

Why like this, why the child? Dr. Kang is still

weeping, but she wants to ask Bullfight what he wants. She goes over the last few years moment by moment, retracing past events, to see if she's done something to Bullfight to make him resentful of her. All she did was work; all she did was brush past him, like always. They didn't even bump into each other all that often, maybe once a quarter, and they rarely exchanged words. When he needled her, she played along or just ignored him. His rudeness was less a reflection of any animosity toward her and more of a huge ego, so she was able to laugh it off. When she considered Bullfight she felt exasperated, as though she were gazing at the youngest son of the family who ruined precariously harmonious dinners before disappearing and then reappearing a couple of times a year to argue and cause trouble. For Hornclaw, who was past the age of holding on to grudges, he had been more like a random passerby. She never thought he was the kind of person she'd befriend in her private life, but for some time she'd at least stopped thinking of him as an imminent threat… At what point did things turn? Was it when she began to gaze at the fruit sellers' granddaughter with delight? Or more precisely, when she began to gaze at Dr. Kang?

She collects herself and folds the paper, then puts it in her bag. "You're right, Dr. Kang. You made the right decision. If you gave this to the police, it might have helped them catch the culprit, but it would have been harder to find your daughter. I'll handle it."

Dr. Kang sucks all the spit in his mouth and expels it forcefully onto the ground. To Hornclaw, this gesture, though out of character for him, isn't threatening; in fact, it's pitiful.

"That's ridiculous," he cries. "I don't know what's going on, but now that I know you're the reason for all of this, I'm going to hand you and the letter over to the police."

"That's fine if that's what you want to do, but your daughter will be in grave danger."

"Okay, fine! If they lay a hand on my daughter, no matter what the laws are, I'll kill you and whoever sent that fax. You can bet that I'll follow you to the ends of the earth and kill you. Nobody has any issue with my family. We're just stuck in the middle of something you're mixed up in. I don't understand why it has to be us. Clearly you're much more than some neighborhood thug. Is it because I shouldn't have saved your life? What was I supposed to do?"

I'm sorry. It's because of me. It's because I was looking at you and went around dribbling my heart from my eyes. Truth be told, I still don't know why that makes you a tar-

get, but that's why Bullfight is annoyed. Hornclaw doesn't say any of that. Instead, she makes a promise.

"I'll find her. I'll bring her back, I will. I know it's hard, but you have to trust me. Don't get the police involved."

"You dragged us into this and now you're giving me orders? This is crazy. I'll have you put behind bars. The fifth? No way. That's two days from now. I don't want her there for another second. You don't want to give back the fax? Fine. I already took a picture of it..."

Even as he babbles on, his face twisted, Dr. Kang never says anything to indicate regret. *I was insane, I shouldn't have saved your life, I should have put you under and called the cops...* That response would've been entirely reasonable, grief-stricken as he is from losing his daughter. His eyes hollow, he just unlocks his cell phone. Hornclaw has seen eyes like this before—the real estate speculator, that client from not long ago. Someone else finished that job and she doesn't know what happened to the client; was she discovered hanging from the ceiling, looking peaceful?

Instinctively Hornclaw kicks Dr. Kang's wrist and sends the cell phone flying ten yards away; she instantly regrets it when she sees the doctor's shocked face. Her reflexes are always a problem. She could have just grabbed and twisted his wrist, or hit the phone out of his grip.

"You're right," she says. "You can expect that a kidnapped child has only seventy-two hours to live. But that's usually the case when it's for a shakedown. Your girl is safe. I know it. You don't have to believe me. But do it my way if you want to see her again. Don't tell your parents, and don't send the cops away, since it'll look suspicious if you suddenly change your behavior. Let them waste their time wiretapping your phone. The police will leave on their own and focus on a different aspect of the investigation. Did they already tap your cell phone?"

Dr. Kang is still in shock. "If they did, would I be here by myself?" he murmurs in resignation. "I'm sure they will if nobody calls the home phone."

"Then go pick up your phone from over there. Nobody's going to call you on that number anyway. She's safe right now." She takes the fax out of her bag and tears off the address, then hands the paper to Dr. Kang. "If the sender of this fax reacts the way I'm suspecting, he'll get rid of her as soon as you show this to the police. But if I go alone, just as he says, she'll be brought back home safely. If she's not back by noon on the sixth, then you're free to do whatever you want.

But wait until then. Don't mess this up by going to this address before the deadline."

She leaves Dr. Kang behind; wretchedness roils in her lungs. Now that things have progressed this far, she won't be able to see him, or his loved ones, again. She shakes off the sadness that settles like dust on her shoulders and gathers rage to fill the emptiness. She holds on to that feeling so that her anger doesn't sour into fear—fear that she won't win against Bullfight.

"You know…" Dr. Kang's hesitant voice tugs at her from behind. "I still don't regret helping you."

Though this begrudging sentence sounds more like he's trying to cast a spell on himself so that he doesn't lose his mind, rather than addressing her, Hornclaw feels buoyant.

"I know," she says. Since it's the last time she'll hear his voice, she takes in his face before she starts walking away, and his expression is more desperate and sorrowful than disgusted, which is a relief. At least that means there's a possibility for change.

But when she's completely out of Dr. Kang's sight, she feels aches in her ankle and pelvis, and she tries to redistribute the heaviness by limping. The pain is so bad that she can't stop the tears.

She takes out her Colt .45, which she hasn't used in a long time but has kept clean and maintained. The maximum effective range would be around forty yards and she can still shoot with one hand, but she's not entirely sure she could hit the mark even if it were closer, say within twenty yards. But would there be a need to attack him from forty yards away? Probably not.

Seven bullets, with one more in the chamber, but she's suddenly concerned that the ammunition is too old. They wouldn't be more than fifteen years old, and since she kept them sealed it's highly unlikely that there would be duds, but in this moment she's worried about all the little problems that could make things go south. Her body may not do what she wants it to.

Everything eventually succumbs to erosion, including the soul. Everything ruptures; possibilities, like aging bodies, wither. The gun is still functioning, but now would be a good time to replace it. She might need an extra firearm, just in case, and her old leather shoulder holster is heavy and cumbersome. She accumulates one excuse after another until she finally decides to visit the middleman who deals in unregulated goods.

She picks up her car keys and, on her way out, looks back at Deadweight, who yawns and pays her no mind. Her water bowl is empty, and she licks the bottom of it, parched. Hornclaw might return home late, so she hangs half a dozen towels soaked in boiling hot water around the apartment and fills the water bowl generously. As soon as she does, Deadweight rushes toward it and sticks her head in the bowl as if she's dying of thirst. She's been neglecting the dog recently, what with the series of distractions that have cropped up, and though she's never taken particularly good care of her, lately it feels as though she's been taking her pet for granted. She's glad that she's at least managed to feed her, dispensing the food automatically like a machine. She checks to make sure the window isn't locked, then closes the front door behind her. After this job is done, as soon as the weather gets nicer, she'll take her out more often. She'll walk her on a leash like every other elderly woman, her steps matching the dog's so that it would be impossible to tell if she is leading the dog or if the dog is leading her. She'll smile at fellow dog walkers. She'll let Deadweight meet other dogs in their neighborhood and give them time to sniff each other. Although perhaps the other dog owners will see she's a mutt and avoid her. What's clear is that Bullfight isn't an easy opponent, which is why the promise of this everyday routine seems to be tempting fate.

The hobby shop doesn't see a lot of foot traffic; most of its customers order online. It more closely resembles a warehouse. Han, whom she called earlier, comes out when he hears the door chime, rubbing his eyes.

"How's your father?" Hornclaw asks.

Han's father is one of her original partners. The elder Han recently began treatment for colorectal cancer, but the treatment is more symbolic. Already seventy-four, the elder Han is physically unwell, unlike Hornclaw who works out constantly, and it's a miracle that he's even managed to survive the surgery. The average life span can't be the yardstick against which to measure an old person's health. The increase in average life expectancy is merely due to the ability of science and medicine to delay death. As the focus is on prolonging life without having fully considered its quality, an old person living in a society with an average life span of one hundred years is like a prophetic shaman who forgets to include "pretty and young" when praying for eternal life and forever ends up with a wrinkly face and a hunched back.

The younger Han seems to want to omit greetings that are irrelevant to their current purpose. "Same as always. Come on in."

In a secluded area of the store he lays out the items she ordered. "Compared to what's being made today, those old leather holsters are really heavy. You can't use that. What are you going to do, march in a parade? This is what people use these days. Do you want a breakfront style? It's secure even when you wear it like this, and it won't slip down. There's a button-release kind, too. You want something that'll be easy for you to use, right?"

Hornclaw touches the nylon holster that Han holds out, then watches as he quickly fills a magazine pouch and takes out a Smith & Wesson 438 and a stun grenade.

"This one was really hard to find. It's about thirty percent smaller than regular grenades, but it performs just as well. It's easier to conceal and throw. I can give you the standard size if you think you might throw it too hard and miss. I have several of those. But if I were you I'd use the small one."

"I'll take the small one. I'm not as strong as I used to be." She smiles, wanting Han to stop talking.

"If you're not as strong as before, you might not want the Colt .45. Even I feel like my arm is going to pop out of the socket when I shoot it. Give me a little more time and I can ask around for a Glock 26 or something else compact."

"I know it's harder to use, but it's what I'm used to. That's what happens when you get old. I don't need anything new. I don't have time, either."

"Then maybe you should take this, the 438. I can understand the holster and the extra firearm, but a stun grenade? Really? Are you planning to mop up guerillas or something?"

"Just give it to me. I don't know what I'm walking into, so it's just as a precaution. I might not need it. Better for me if I don't end up using it." She puts the gift box Han has wrapped in her shoulder bag, and holds out an envelope of cash.

Han opens the envelope and his eyes widen. "Thank you, but this is too much."

"I'm sorry I haven't been to visit your father. Add it to your dad's health care costs. Just tell him hello for me."

Only then does Han look regretful that he batted away her greeting earlier. "He's still all there. It would be nice if you could visit him in person."

"That might be hard to schedule. But tell him I asked after him."

Looking relieved that extra cash has fallen into his lap, Han bids her goodbye, bowing his head awkwardly.

That evening, she calls Worryfixer. She can't tell from their voice if the agency knows about this new development, but judging from how sloppy Sohn is, he probably didn't do any vetting once the deposit was wired over. For a short moment she wonders if Bullfight and the agency are in bed together, using this opportunity to dispatch the useless old lady who gets in the way. What a good excuse that would be, since her mistake caused damage to the agency's reputation—but Bullfight isn't the type to take on work like that, and more importantly, there would be no reason to make it such an inefficient, complicated process when it would be simpler to eliminate her without all this drama. Before she hangs up, Hornclaw tells Worryfixer that she will give them a call afterward, since it will be hard for her to answer the phone when she's on the job. She then disconnects all the ways the agency could get in touch with her. She forces herself to eat a few spoons of mixed-grain rice and seaweed soup as a late dinner, then takes Deadweight to the bathroom to give her a long, careful bath for the first time in a while. The dog, who dislikes the shower, shakes the water off.

She skips her cup of coffee so that she can sleep deeply, but she still ends up tossing and turning, going over what's in store for the next day. Perhaps out of consideration for her owner, Deadweight goes out to the living room instead of crawling into her bed. Hornclaw counts sheep jumping over a fence, even picturing the texture of the sheep's wool, one strand at a time, as she tries to force herself asleep.

Though there's plenty of time until she is to appear—it would take no more than five hours to get to the destination no matter how bad traffic is, as she figured out after a GPS-guided practice run, closer to four hours even when she takes into account possible delays—Hornclaw's eyes fly open at seven in the morning. Even so, she's overslept because she had a hard time falling asleep; she usually wakes at five thirty. But she thinks he would have arrived early, so she packs her bag and straps on all her gear, then fills Deadweight's food bowl, just in case, and strokes her sleeping head.

"I'll be back. Sleep well, and guard the place."

She's stunned by the chill under her hand. The dog's fur is lusterless. She didn't notice it earlier, but when she sniffs she smells something out of the ordinary. Deadweight is lying on her side and dark watery waste has spread out under her body. She places a finger on the dog's neck and presses harder, then sits dejectedly in front of the body for a long time, her hand still against her neck. Deadweight's body is heavy when she gently shakes her.

So strange how the body grows heavier once the soul leaves, even though that's the part that takes up the most space.

She pulls herself up, locks the window and leaves.

She gets off the highway at the first rest area and looks for a pay phone. There's only one that works properly, since everyone uses cell phones these days. She doesn't know how much a call costs anymore or how many coins she'll need, so she brings a fistful in her pocket and begins to dial.

The first is a wrong number. A woman's voice she's never heard before answers. Hornclaw regrets disabling all of her communication devices; she's even shattered her cell phone. She tries her best to remember the correct number. She tries numbers that glimmer faintly in her mind, changing the order, and only when her pocket is feeling lighter does she realize that the first number was the right one.

"Who was that? Not your wife, was she? I wasted a ton of coins."

"None of your business," grumbles Choi, the caretaker at the memorial park. "What's going on? I'm off today. Did you really need to call on my day off?"

"I have a favor to ask."

"If you're asking for a favor it can't be something pleasant. Can't it wait?" Choi's voice is sullen.

"This is the only bit of spare time I have. It's not terribly urgent, but could you do it by tomorrow at the latest? You know where I live, right? Go there, and look for a flat rock on the second step of the stairs. It's on the right side. Lift it up and you'll find a key."

Hornclaw needs to draw a deep breath to prepare herself for what she's about to say next. Whenever she thinks about Deadweight, even in passing, she recalls the remodeled kitchen window, the bottom of the bowl that always has dried food stuck on it, the clumps of brown fur that tickle her nose every time the dog shakes her body, and these images always make her heart ache.

"Inside you'll find a dog lying in the living room. Thanks in advance."

Even though she doesn't describe what happened,

Choi, with his professional instincts, understands immediately, and his voice turns warmer. "Oh, no, poor
thing. I didn't know you were raising a dog! Did you
have to send it off to go on a difficult job?"

"I wasn't raising her, I was just beside her. I didn't
kill her, it was just her time. I think she lived out her
natural life. I'm calling you because I don't have time
to bring her to you."

"I understand. It's no problem, as long as it's not
today. And the bill?"

"I'll call you later. If you don't hear from me in
three days, you can settle it with Worryfixer. They'll
be able to handle it."

A warning beep goes off and the call ends before
she can hear Choi's answer. She's out of coins; her
pocket is empty. Even though it's only coins she's de-
pleted, Hornclaw feels as if she's discarding one thing
after another from her shabby life.

An abandoned taupe building holds up the sky, pregnant with snow.

There would be no reason for him to command her to meet in the middle of a busy city street if the purpose was to make her run futile errands, so she was prepared for what the location would be like. But even she didn't think it would be such a bleak, unsightly place. At the unfamiliar address is a half-built building. Judging from the design, it appears to have been planned as an apartment building, but construction has been halted, with only the outer walls and frame standing—it's long been abandoned. Someone must have decided to build apartments out here in the wilderness, or maybe someone was scammed and went bankrupt. Even if the building was completed it would have had serious problems, as the lot appears to have been made by flattening part of the surrounding hills, making it unsafe during a heavy downpour.

Back when she and Ryu were working together, spaces like these were strewn everywhere just outside the city center. But she has no idea how the kid found a place like this in this day and age. It's the kind of place where you could dispose of a corpse in broad daylight. All around her are empty hills and frozen fields and paddies. About fifty yards away from the hills is a single-story building that appears to be a small factory, but the doors are closed tightly. She would have to drive for at least half an hour to see another human being or find a store that's open.

She turns the car off and gingerly approaches the abandoned building surrounded by long weeds, dry dust blooming behind her footsteps.

A vine is coiled around a sign; she squints to read it.

Notice
Work on this construction site has been halted. For your safety, do not enter. Trespassers may be prosecuted.

Hornclaw is wearing only a cotton shirt under a stiff jacket and the wind scrapes her dry skin. She hasn't done anything yet, but she can hear every joint in her body creak. Her heart is already numb. She grits her teeth and climbs the cement stairs silently, one step at a time. Concrete has been poured over the frame of the abandoned building, but it's exposed to the elements, and the discolored outer walls are surrounded by scaffolding that looks like it's ready to crumble at first touch. Workers must have stopped in the middle of dismantling it, or maybe parts had eroded and fallen off over time. Inside, there's nothing that could provide cover; no matter where she looks, all she sees are pillars holding up gray walls and ceiling, along with open rectangles that would have become windows.

She closes her eyes for a second by the stairs, then focuses, listening for any noise, her footsteps silent. She begins to perspire, and a cold bead of sweat coasts down her cheek and follows the curve of her earlobe; then she senses the vibration of a gun cocking, reflexively moves aside and sees the bullet strike the wall where she was just standing. Gray dust billows.

She darts back down the steps and a couple of shots ring out behind her, causing the pillars to puff with dust. She doesn't hear anyone running down after her; the assailant must be waiting for her to come up, coolly preparing to drill bullets into her head.

So it can't be Bullfight. Right now, for whatever

reason, he's eager to peacock around, so it's hard to imagine him staying hidden like a sharpshooter. He must have hired specialists who are out of work during the slow season. How many were there? If one person was on each floor, there couldn't be more than five total. In a quickly formed team without special forces backgrounds, someone will always be out of sync, but these shooters are patiently lying low; they are likely highly trained soldiers.

A child's cries ring out from somewhere; the girl is probably thoroughly terrified by the shots. Hornclaw sprints out of the building on the tips of her toes, then, outside, looks up to figure out what floor the sound is coming from, but she can't hear a thing; maybe they clamped a hand over her mouth or knocked her out. But it didn't sound like the child is above the seventh floor.

The Colt in her right hand, she climbs up a big dying tree next to the building. All the muscles in her body are screaming, the bare branches seem to be on the verge of snapping in half, and she can't be any quieter because there aren't any leaves to muffle the sound. But at least the noise is mixed in with the wind shaking the tree. There's someone on the second floor, but he seems to be focused on the center stairwell, and when she looks into the third-floor window, she can see the back of the head of a man, pacing, waiting for her.

She collects her breath and lifts her arm. *You can do it. Place your pointer finger there. Just to the middle of the first joint. No, no, if you go all the way to the second joint the bullet will lurch up or veer to the left. One more time. No, no, the whole first joint. Don't put the tip of your finger on it gently like that. It'll lean to the right. Exactly in the middle. Right, just like that.*

She aims at his head as he wanders by, completely unaware of her presence; then he walks slowly back toward her and looks up absentmindedly, his eyes meeting hers, and before he can raise his gun she calmly pulls the trigger. The bullet pitches inside the barrel and she feels it burst out, the force of the release moving from her wrist to her elbow as it spreads into pain and pressure, as if her shoulder is being dislocated, and, as she hears the man scream, she sees a red hole in his head beyond the sight.

She throws a rope around the outer pillar and swiftly shimmies over to land in the building; she hears the others scurrying after hearing the gunshot and the victim's scream. The men must be surprised that the scream is not a woman's because they scatter. This is more of a ragtag group than she initially thought. A wise operative would hide and stay quiet at a time like this, but one is running up from the second floor while another dashes down from the fourth. The cadence and speed of their footsteps suggest that they will arrive on the third floor at the same time. She's standing by the staircase, plastered to the wall, and pulls out the other gun from her hip holster, shooting in both directions at nearly the same time, and the split second between the two shots is what causes different results, with the man below grazed by the bullet and dropping his gun while the one above, hit square in the center of his abdomen, tumbles down the stairs, huge quantities of blood spraying in an arc until he stops at her feet. The man below takes out another gun and is about to shoot, but she slips off her jacket and throws it at him as she leaps aside, covering his field of vision, then shoots him in the head through her jacket.

She picks up her jacket and puts it back on, then glances down at the first floor. The gun dropped by the operative is down there. He's prone on the floor, not moving. The man shot in the stomach writhes, and she shoots him twice more, flips him over with her foot, puts his Beretta in her shoulder holster and straps her other gun to her hip. It's not ideal to carry more weight, but she doesn't know how many men remain; brighter ones might be hiding on their floors.

Although this site is remote and abandoned, it's not a hunting area and there have already been too many gunshots. Though it's winter, there could be a small temple in the hills somewhere, and even if she assumes that Bullfight has already scoped out the area for such possibilities, there could always be a few wild-ginseng hunters out; she can't waste too much time. Since her opponent is entirely unhinged, she doesn't think he'll care that the sound of gunfire could reach houses nearby, as he could just take the child and leave if he finds himself in a compromising situation, but with all that said, it will be hard for the child to survive much longer in a concrete building open to the elements. Though they say that children, who tend to have higher baseline temperatures and expend less energy than grown-ups, is more likely to survive than adults if stranded in the snowy mountains, that doesn't mean the girl will experience less pain. Since she's not making any sound now, she has to be tied up or maybe unconscious, and if the latter, in this frigid cold her body temperature will nosedive. Hornclaw has to get to the child as quickly as possible.

But she can't let impatience jeopardize the goal. She can't open her mouth and call for Bullfight. She can't demand that he reveal himself, that they have a fair fight. If she does, he'll detect the desperation and anxiety gushing out of her. It's not that she is too proud to reveal her fear; it's that Bullfight might jeer at her terror and twist Haeni's neck right then and there.

She grabs on to the scaffolding and pulls herself up. Hanging from the outer wall, she climbs up to the fourth floor, and when she looks around quickly she doesn't see anyone; she's already shot the operative stationed there in the stomach. Before she can get safely up to the fifth floor, the scaffolding creaks and clangs, and an arm emerges from the fifth floor to fire at her. The bullets hit the scaffolding, which is held together precariously, as she throws herself into the building. Four more shots, and she rolls behind a pillar, but a bullet has flung off her hat and another has ripped through her left sleeve. The operative rushes toward her but trips on the rope she throws at him, and his shot misses and strikes the wall. He's focused on getting himself disentangled, swearing all the while, so when she leaps out from behind the pillar the operative reacts too late and misses. The bullet tears through the fluttering hood of her jacket, and she shoots him in the forehead.

Another head. Three heads, four men. She wasn't all that fixated on heads, but at this moment she thinks of Ryu; perhaps this tendency to continuously recall the past means her own death is imminent. *Always the head. It's better than the gut, which might be behind a bulletproof vest. Of course, it depends where in the head. They don't die instantly if the spinal cord or brain stem isn't destroyed, but it's still the best way to stop them from moving. Shooting them in the heart or the stomach is less effective because of the sheer number of bullets you'll have to use. It's hard to hit and even harder to kill instantly. Always go for the head when you're shooting from a distance, and go for the limbs when you're fighting in close quarters. Think about how someone will feel when he sees that his wrist has been shot off. That's way more effective in damaging their psyche than when they're on the ground, bleeding from the stomach. Even if he doesn't bleed out, he might die from shock anyway.* But as they emerged from the wilderness and hunting grounds and moved more frequently in crowded cities, they used guns much less; their clients tended not to prefer it.

Now she's using a gun for the first time in nearly a decade, and things aren't as they were before, from her physicality to everything else. She's panting already and she's aching everywhere as if pebbles were raked across her skin. She's bleeding from her left arm, which she can't feel due to the cold, and she misses Ryu. She's been putting off joining him all this time because there was no special reason for it, but today it feels like she can't delay it any longer.

She pulls a handkerchief out of a pocket of her cargo pants and ties up her arm, then hears a whine and a dull thud, over and over again, louder and louder. It's coming from above.

She points her gun toward the stairs, then her jaw drops open. A thick sack is rolling horizontally down the stairs. Bullfight is pushing the sack with his feet. She hears muffled cries from inside. A man, perhaps the last hired gun, follows Bullfight down the stairs, his firearm aimed at the sack, ready for Hornclaw to make a move.

"Don't kick her!" she yells, her gun still aiming up, but her voice wavers.

"I'm not you, am I?" Bullfight kicks the sack as hard as he can from a few steps above the landing.

The sack hurtles toward her knees, and she falls back, supporting the child with the tops of her feet. Of course she didn't have the chance to pull the trigger. Before Hornclaw can get up, the operative aims his gun at her head.

"I thought I was going to die of boredom," Bullfight remarks. "So you finally made me come downstairs? You don't deserve your name. You were just looking around doing nothing. Is this kid that important? Here I am, coming down unarmed, and there you are, hesitating, not shooting, and look where that's landed you."

"So this was what you wanted to show me? A pathetic sideshow?"

"Of course not. I wanted to welcome you with more fanfare, but I don't have an unlimited budget." Lit by the afternoon sunlight, Bullfight's smile sharpens and turns peculiar. "And it wouldn't be fun if you ended up dying before you even found me. So. Are you warmed up now?"

The operative, who looked reluctant all along, pauses at this and glares at Bullfight. "Are you serious? After all that? Warmed up? Who do you think you—"

"Do you have a problem? You got paid up front."

The operative is starting to get enraged by Bullfight's snark, and Hornclaw tuts inwardly and starts to pull her feet out from under the sack, little by little so that she won't be noticed. *Just as I thought. They're not in sync.*

"So what?" the operative snaps. "Everyone's dead thanks to your stupid antics. If I shoot this lady in the head, do I get the other guys' payment?"

Bullfight smirks derisively. "You knew you were cannon fodder when I paid you that much. It just goes to show how lame you guys are."

The operative suddenly swings the gun around to aim at Bullfight, and as he pulls the trigger, Hornclaw shoots him through the wrist. The operative drops his gun, forcing the bullet to pierce the stairs instead of Bullfight's head. Swearing, he launches himself at her, a knee to her shoulder, and twists her wrist to grab her gun, with which he strikes her on the forehead. The world spins in front of her eyes as he gets up; he is about to kick her in the stomach but she rolls away. His shrieks shake the empty concrete building; it's because she's slashed both his ankles with her Buck knife as she spun away. Howling, he jams the gun into her face and pulls the trigger, but he's out of bullets.

"Fuck!"

She never filled the chamber with the last bullet.

The operative flings the gun away and Bullfight laughs, bending over in exaggerated mirth. "How many times did I tell you? She's not easy."

He gazes at her with something like admiration as she wobbles to her feet, about to keel over, even though she's somehow managed not to drop her knife.

"I know you worked hard, so when I'm back in Seoul I'll make sure you get your due," Bullfight says to the operative. "But will you be able to drive? Here, I'll give you the car keys. Your hands and feet are all busted and you can't shoot anymore, so you're not useful to me, got it? And this granny over here isn't the type to track you down and kill you. So take the keys and go on, if you're so worried about your life."

The operative seems not to have a spare weapon—or perhaps he's lost his fighting spirit from the severe bleeding and pain—so he picks up the car keys Bullfight dropped on the floor and glares hatefully at Hornclaw before crawling down the stairs like a wriggling caterpillar. It looks like it'll take him nearly all day to go down all five stories.

By the time Hornclaw pulls herself together, Bullfight has already opened the sack and taken the child out; she wonders if she could have gotten to the child if she had gritted her teeth and moved faster even after she was bashed in the head, but concludes that she wouldn't have been able to. Even though Bullfight kicked the girl all the way to her feet, she wasn't able to use that opportunity to her benefit. The Colt clattered down the stairs when the operative threw it aside; with her knife still in her hand, she takes out the Beretta she collected downstairs and aims at Bullfight's chest, but what she sees is the fear-soaked child's face. Haeni is wearing a red coat that appears to be new, and her hands and feet are bound. Bullfight has one arm around the girl's neck and the other hand holds a paring knife with a curved blade. It's only about three inches long end to end, but it wouldn't be too hard to slice off a child's small, soft, apricot-hued ear, which has turned a terrified blue in the cold air.

From this distance she knows she can shoot him in the head. Except the child's ear won't emerge intact. Is it the right thing to do, to sacrifice an ear to get the child back? She wouldn't hesitate if it were an adult, and what she knows is how to kill, not how to save someone, but there's also no guarantee that the asshole would only slice off the ear as he's shot. She fights the intense animalistic instinct to rush at him, to smash that rude piece of shit's jaw, regardless of Haeni; then she vaguely remembers how in similar circumstances when things went wrong, she set aside the well-being of the hostage and shot her foe the way Ryu taught her. But then Dr. Kang's rage and tears rush to her head.

She wouldn't have known her heart's capacity for pain if she hadn't witnessed Dr. Kang's reaction. Things she never thought were meaningful once Ryu was gone. And this all leads to the sensation of Deadweight's dull fur, cold under her hand.

She tosses down the Beretta and the knife. "Let her go."

"So you're not senile yet, seeing how you fully understand the situation. Get rid of the one you have on your hip, too."

She takes off the hip holster and throws it down. "Let's hear it. What's your problem with me, anyway?"

"If you can't think of it on your own, there's no point in telling you." He sounds serious.

Hornclaw snorts. Why is she looking for reason and logic from an unhinged kid? "Whatever. What do I need to do for you to send her back?"

She believed too simply that what Bullfight wants from her is a sign of defeat. Perhaps she can signal her submission by kneeling or something; he seems annoyed by the fact that she's a woman, an old woman at that, and someone who used to be renowned for her skills.

"Why do you think it's up to me to send her back? It's easier if you defeat me and just take her."

Defeat him?

That would be near impossible to do, but she gamely picks up her knife. She still doesn't understand what game he's trying to play with her, but he seems to want it to be more dramatic and violent than a simple kill. Bullfight pushes Haeni down against a pillar, her hands and feet still bound, and he's now holding a military-grade Gerber knife. The paring knife is nowhere to be seen; perhaps he's tucked it away.

"All right if I kill you?" Her voice is shaking.

Bullfight notices and stifles a smile. "Wasn't that your plan all along?" Suddenly his voice is right by her ear, not across the way. Somehow he's already next to her. She feels a sharp throbbing along her cheekbone; blood is seeping out. She's reflexively knocked the knife away, changing the direction of the blade; the original target seems to have been her forehead, and if he'd succeeded, it would have been hard for her to see clearly through the gushing blood.

Haeni's weeping sounds like it's echoing from far away, not coming from the pillar right in front of her. Hornclaw lunges to stab Bullfight low in the ribs, but she doesn't make contact; the handle of his knife slams down on her back as he kicks her behind the knees. She yelps and tumbles to the ground, unable to move.

Bullfight looks down at her and sighs. "I stopped at tripping you out of respect for senior citizens. Why are you howling like that? You're acting like your ligaments have ruptured." He steps back and pulls the girl's hair to raise her head. "If you don't make it fun for me, I'll just toss her out the window."

Hornclaw leans on her good knee to get up, but crumples to the floor at the sound of a huge explosion. She looks out to see black, billowing smoke. The child manages to swallow her sobs and sucks in her snot. The car and the operative have exploded, a bomb attached to the engine igniting when the car was sufficiently warmed up.

"Oh no," Bullfight says, not sounding at all sorry. "We have even less time now with all this commotion."

"What have you... Was this the plan from the beginning?" Hornclaw sputters, the stench of burning human flesh assaulting her nose.

"I guess whoever wins can drive back in your car," Bullfight says casually.

He's about to fling the child back down, but notices that her hair is tangled in the band of his wristwatch, so he slices a hank of hair off. Haeni squirms, trying to get away. Bullfight is no longer paying attention to the girl, and Hornclaw spots the child inching away, bit by bit, and, relieved that the girl has the will to move, uses her wrist to block the knife coming at her. Blood sprays from her slashed wrist and she turns to the side to duck the blade aiming at her carotid artery, then stabs him in the thigh. She senses his strong, taut leg muscle clenching the blade. He turns and smashes her in the face, and she falls, missing her chance to pull her knife out. It takes her a while to recover from the pain between her eyes and in her hip, and by the time she gets to her feet, he's managed to pull the knife out of his thigh, severing his leg's lateral muscles.

"A present for me?" he asks.

She watches him twirl the bloodied knives as if they are featherlight and pulls out her backup knife from a side pocket. It's only about two-thirds the length of Bullfight's knife, and it's the last weapon she has. The rope and the stun grenade are in the pouch she's cast off. Not that they would be all that useful in this situation anyway. Though she's still wobbly on her feet, her stance shows her readiness.

Bullfight limps toward her slowly, trying to find a weak spot. "Well, I'm at an advantage, aren't I? Should I get rid of one of these?"

"If you want. You'll regret it, though." Before she even finishes speaking, her own Buck knife is spiraling toward her eyes. She leaps back, thinking she's managed to avoid it, but realizes it's stuck in her thigh.

"There you go," Bullfight says.

"Thanks."

Injuries always accompany this line of work, but the shot of icy pain that twists in her leg makes her catch her breath. She gets used to the sensation, breathes deeply and yanks the knife out, tossing the smaller one aside. Since it was thrown into her leg, her injury isn't as deep as Bullfight's.

Meanwhile, Haeni has reached the stairwell. She could go down one step at a time even though she's tied up, but she has no idea where the stairs might lead. That's when she discovers a cell phone, its screen scratched and shattered—it must have slipped out of the operative's pocket. Haeni uses her lips to press the home button, slides to unlock it, and since she doesn't know the passcode, she touches Emergency. The car is still burning outside, and the scary man and the weak-looking grandma are taunting each other and screaming, slashing at each other. Haeni dials, then bends over to place her ear against the phone. When someone answers, she forgets that she's been crying and calmly explains what's going on. The fact that she's saying she was kidnapped and giving them her dad's cell phone number should speed things up, but the operator is having a hard time believing what the child is reporting and asks the same questions over and over again.

Meanwhile, Bullfight slashes Hornclaw below her collarbone, causing her to crumple to the floor, then discovers what the child is doing and stalks over to snatch the phone away from her. He throws the phone against the wall and a split second before he is about to slash the girl's face, Hornclaw stabs him. Screaming, Haeni squirms away and tumbles down a few steps, and Bullfight lunges at Hornclaw, who twists and blocks his arm. But she gets a cut on her chin, she's losing quite a lot of blood from the wound below her collarbone, and everything is turning fuzzy. The police are bound to be on their way now that the car has detonated, but Bullfight seems unconcerned; he appears almost deranged as he toys with her. She tries to block his quick jabs and thrusts, concerned about what will happen to the girl if she's killed before help arrives. Dr. Kang might already be on his way—all Haeni has to do is hang on until her dad and the police arrive, but since they're in the middle of nowhere, it's going to take time even if the local police are dispatched first. Hornclaw feels her body growing heavier by the minute, and senses that she exists solely to distract Bullfight. She hasn't been able to buy enough time, she thinks, and that's when Bullfight's knife sinks deep under her ribs.

"What are you doing, standing there stupidly like that?" Bullfight is starting to get angry, having glimpsed in her eyes the will to drag this on for as long as possible rather than to win. He's insulted, but at the same time a silent emptiness fills his heart. As that hollowness takes hold, he senses something leaking out of him. Overwhelmed with rage, he decides it's time to kill Hornclaw and cut the girl's throat. It would be too banal for Hornclaw to die from all the small cuts that now cover her body.

He swings his knife straight up, but she kneels back, and his blade swipes air. She stabs him in the lower abdomen and drags her knife up near his liver, causing Bullfight to topple over onto her. A bystander might think they are lovers embracing, not in the throes of a grisly fight.

Hornclaw is so weak she can barely bend a finger, but she doesn't want to be discovered as a corpse under Bullfight of all people, so she manages to flip him over and push him off. The tang of death wafts from his abdomen and his intestines are visible, even through the blood. She tilts him on his side and props his head up with her balled-up jacket, so that he won't choke on his own blood, which he's vomiting up. It would be meaningless to ask him if she should call the ambulance. She tries to grip her Buck knife properly to end his suffering when his bloodied hand rests on her wrist.

"Don't. Leave me be."

She hesitates but folds her knife away. "Don't worry. I'll be following right behind you." This is what she didn't get to say to Ryu back then.

Bullfight's eyes are still open, but his breathing turns shallow, and she can't tell if he is smiling or if it's an involuntary twitch right before death. It's the first time she's stared at him from up close, but his blood-splattered face contains hints of anger and mischief and mystery. Looking down at him, she has an unexpected thought—maybe she could have met this boy in another place, in another way, in another guise.

And then instead of slashing at each other's throats, perhaps they would have embraced each other.

Without thinking, she murmurs, "It's you," as absentmindedly as though she's stepping on tender, gentle blades of grass in the forest.

She sees his eyes opening gradually.

"You remember?"

She doesn't know what made her say that. She doesn't know what he means; was she wandering through a memory just now? Should she ask him what he means? A shadow darkens her heart, conjuring memories and releasing locked-up words. She's killed so many people that she can't begin to count each one; maybe the kid is related to one of them, or maybe he has nothing to do with any of them. As she steps closer to Ryu's world, the individual flakes of those memories don't have any meaning to her. She considers herself someone who doesn't deserve to wallow in memories or to feel them or drink them in. Though for Bullfight, that memory, whatever it may be, seems to be important even in this moment, when the vast eternity is gaping before him.

"How did you know?" he asks.

She can't bring herself to tell him that she doesn't remember. "The clarity, right? You know how they say that some things suddenly dawn on you when you're about to meet your end."

From her demeanor, Bullfight realizes she hasn't remembered anything. He's merely one of countless young children left behind as she swept through their lives. But he doesn't reveal his disappointment. "Okay, then."

Okay—because it wouldn't be possible for all of those children to search for her, and it would be even rarer for any of them to breathe their last breath beside her. Bullfight taps her knee.

"My head."

It becomes easier to breathe when she props his head on her knee. He knows that this momentary comfort, a dot in the middle of his expansive pain, is the inevitable process of crossing over to the other side. What parts of his life would flash by him now? All the experiences he's had, all the choices he's made, all the people he's killed—they unspool in front of him. It's like a videotape where you can stick your finger in the hole and pull out the contents, but there is only one scene from his memories that he can hold on to.

"You said things dawn on you when it's time for you to go?" Bullfight joggles his chin and grins, and the blood pooled in his mouth trickles out. "So that means it's not your time yet."

The grassy smell grows faint and disappears.

Hornclaw closes Bullfight's eyes. She murmurs absently, "And are you able to swallow pills now?"

Declaring that he used to be the principal of a public high school that sent the most students to Seoul National University, an impossible feat these days for any school that isn't specialized or private, the old man insists that no other public school has topped his track record. The man sitting next to him claims that the former principal is exaggerating, that it happened just one year, and snorts that this is the thousandth time he has had to suffer through that damn boasting. The two aren't friends, rather they are like most of the elderly men in this park who made acquaintances as they come and go. The men here generally let the others boast in exchange for talking at length about themselves, but among them there is always a stub-

born one who has to get the last word in. The second
man could have let go of the issue once the former
principal quieted down, but he goes on, pointing out
that the other man had to find work as an apartment
building security guard after retirement and then had
been driven out of that job by the women's association because of his incessant moralizing and boasting. This man, a former marine, is proud that he's
well versed in how things have changed and claims
to be open-minded, but since he's open-minded in
a selective way this trait actually makes him one of
the most exhausting types. After leaving the marine
corps he ran a large aquaculture business, which he
had to close after two fires and a disastrous cold spell
that killed all the fish, and while the correlation between his military service and his former business is
not entirely clear, he emphasizes at every opportunity
that he's a former marine and that he applies discipline
to everything he does, his hectoring tone the same as
that of the former principal.

A handful of old men are sitting around them, but
nobody intervenes. Soon the argument between the
former principal and the former marine grows heated;
a soju bottle flies and breaks, sending shards of glass
slicing through the air, glinting in the late afternoon
sunlight, before skittering along the ground. These

bored old men can fight over a boast as small as a square of toilet paper. Stories with just a dash of sugar expand like cotton candy until they end up soggy and sticky.

Under a tree, two old men sitting on backless benches across a rented Go board, clacking pieces, are competing over which of them is being treated more disrespectfully by their son's families, who they both live with, and as their conversation meanders from the government's depleting pension system to politics before concluding that young people pay attention only if their faces are on fire, the outcome of the game becomes irrelevant.

On the next bench over, a man in a traditional coat is reading the newspaper through a magnifying glass, glancing at an old woman sitting across the way who is aggressively rummaging through her handbag with just one hand. She's wearing an embroidered hat over her attractively dyed brown hair, so he can't immediately discern her true age, and though her attire is elegant he thinks she must be one of those middle-aged sex workers who approach old men with the pretense of selling health drinks, just dressed a little nicer. He gets up to sit next to her and settles so close to her that her elbow bumps him, and she scoots away, making the old man feel embarrassed.

"Have you lost something?" the old man asks, truly believing that a health tonic would appear out of her bag after all that rummaging.

The old woman looks up, as though unsure whether he is addressing her, before replying. "Yes, well, it looks like I left my phone at home."

"Who would make an urgent call to old people like us?"

"I suppose that's true, but I have to cancel an appointment. Take care."

She stands up, and the breeze flutters one empty sleeve of her dark blue chiffon blouse and her animal-print scarf. She hurries away; the old man tuts in disappointment.

The nail shop owner, who is in her fifties, is slightly on edge. She's hired a twenty-two-year old with a level two license as a favor to a client, and the girl has been ridiculous since day one. In addition to the instructions given at the end of the interview, the owner added just one more thing to her list, to clean the shop after closing, and now the girl is saying she can't do it, insisting that someone with a license should be able to see clients right away. She claims she shouldn't have to come in early to observe the more experienced staff, as she doesn't have anything more to learn, and even if she did she wouldn't grow in her career by doing the work of apprentices, cleaning and laundering towels. At first, the owner figured that the new girl didn't know how things worked in the real world and wasn't clued in on how to be respectful since she'd never held a job before. In reality, it's the exact opposite, with the girl confidently declaring that it's a matter of workers' rights, and that even if the employer ordered her to do something, she shouldn't be expected to do it just for the sake of custom or tradition if it was beyond her job duties. The owner made a comment half in jest, *Aren't you so brave when the youth unemployment rate is so high?* The girl went on about how there should be legislation outlawing unjust practices particularly when the youth are struggling, shocking the owner, who learned her trade through abusive apprenticeships. How would this girl manage to keep even a part-time job with her refusal to do the tiniest bit of extra work? If it were up to the owner, she would tell the girl to get lost, but she seems to be the kind of person who would instantly petition the labor ministry and make a huge stink, and anyway, the owner has to think about the client who recommended the girl. It's thanks to that client, who brought models and corporate executives to the shop, that they have a roster of around fifty regulars; that's why she doesn't have low seasons and sees consistent sales. Feeling that she was doing a good deed, the owner explained patiently that while that might be correct in principle, if independent businesses followed the letter of the law they would all have to close. While a smaller operation may quickly want to promote apprentices, the situation at this shop, devoted to the artistry of nail decor and welcoming a thousand regulars, was different; since there were already an assistant, a head assistant and a manager above the new girl, she should assist them, watching and learning the basics of how to work with clients before coming face-to-face with clients of her own. She attempted to persuade the new girl by saying, "A license just means you have the skills, and you need more than skills to satisfy customers". This made the new girl shed copious tears, saying that she didn't pay all that money to learn nail art just to be treated so poorly, suddenly turning into the victim, so the owner, at the end of her rope, allowed the new girl to take a client who made an appointment for the following day. Judging from the voice over the phone, the client seemed to be an older woman who sounded apprehensive. The owner, a veteran businesswoman of nearly thirty years, concluded that she wasn't that economically comfortable, rarely had her nails done before, and didn't seem like someone who would post a negative review online, making her the perfect client for the new girl.

But the client in question kept calling the shop this morning, saying she didn't think it would suit her and wanted to cancel, then dialing ten minutes later to say she changed her mind and would in fact keep her appointment, then calling again to cancel. The owner figured it just came with the territory for an elderly customer who had never gotten her nails done, but the new girl, who was the one answering the phone, finally snapped in irritation at the fourth call, saying, "Can't you just make a decision? Do you understand that you're being a nuisance?" Horrified, the owner yanked the phone out of the girl's hand and convinced the client to come in, saying that nail art only lasts two weeks at most so there was no need to agonize over it. You can think of it as something women do as a diversion, she explained, and offered a special discount to apologize for the new employee, who was still just learning.

The client who finally walks in is elderly and very small; though she's dressed nicely she seems low-spirited and her skin tone is uneven. If they put nail tips on and painted them, her hands would pop unnaturally. The moment she sees the old lady, the owner gets it—this woman isn't a retired CEO or a professional;

she's not focused on her appearance, and she's not the type to parade around dinner parties with a wineglass, showing off her nails and jewelry. She seems uncomfortable, as if she's begrudgingly getting her nails done for a friend's son's wedding. She could have gone into any nail place in her neighborhood; why did she come all the way downtown? That's a frequent rookie mistake made by matrons who have enough money to spend but don't know what's appropriate.

The owner nudges the new girl, who looks as if she's stepped in shit, and reminds her to guide the client to select a simple, one-color style. This old lady is perfect for the new girl to practice on.

But even with these precise instructions, the new girl holds the client's right hand in hers, and, perhaps impassioned by her chance to take care of a real client, or wanting to show off her overflowing talents, begins to talk about things this client won't even begin to understand. She goes on about cuticle care, the option to put stones on the tips, the benefits of silk nail wraps and gradient nails, and then notes that the client's hands need a basic treatment procedure. The owner wonders if she should intervene but decides to be compassionate, understanding that the new girl would want to obtain a regular and brag about it. Then the client asks tartly, "My hands need a basic treatment procedure? Does this shop do procedures? It's just maintenance, isn't it? Is there a dermatologist here? Do you realize it's illegal for you to do any procedures?"

Though the client didn't look like she would understand the difference between a procedure and maintenance, she's now being testy and cranky; the owner finally jumps in. "Ma'am, she's just trying to make it easy to understand. Generally we call it hand and nail care."

The new girl regains her confidence and adds, "Yes, that's right. Hand and nail care. But we can certainly skip that part if you want. And even if you don't choose to do it, basic care is included in all services, like trimming your nails and cuticles. And if you would like to get nail art, it's actually better to skip more specialized care, because then it can trap moisture between your nails and the tips. If you want nail art, but they tell you to do care first—well, that happens only at shops that don't have a lot of experience. I was just letting you know about all these options, and while I recommend doing things in the proper order, it's of course up to you, ma'am."

"Then let's just do that art thing or whatever it is. Since it's supposed to be a hundred thousand won with the discount, let's keep it to that. You can pick the method and color and shape. And let me make it clear. Don't call me ma'am. Do you call all older customers ma'am?"

The owner tries to smooth over the situation. "I'm so sorry. Please forgive us. Please choose the design you'd like from these samples."

With that, the owner gives up trying to control the new girl, though it's also partly because her VIP client walks in just then to be escorted into a private room.

After a long session focused on the VIP's hand and nail care, the owner pops out to tell the new girl to bring in some tea, but sees the senior assistant and the manager huddled around the sniffling girl in the empty shop.

"What's going on?"

"We were busy with our own clients and didn't pay enough attention, and it turns out she didn't charge that old lady enough. It's ridiculous."

"What happened? Did you paint her nails properly? Didn't I tell you to stick to just one color and keep it simple?" Sighing, the owner figures that the prickly old lady must have complained about the color or the stones, causing the new girl to give her an additional discount without asking, and vows to take it out of her pay.

But what the new girl says next surprises her.

"Yes, she liked it. I worked so hard on it. And I know you said it was a hundred thousand won with the discount. But when we were talking earlier, I was holding just her right hand so I didn't know."

Here, the girl draws in a deep, wobbly breath, making an expression as if she'd suffered through the worst hardship in the world in those measly thirty minutes.

"I was doing basic care, and that's when I realized she doesn't have a left hand. At all. She doesn't have ten fingers, she has just five. So when she was leaving, I only charged her half. Fifty thousand won. Is that so wrong? A client with only one hand comes in to make that one hand look pretty, and I charge her based on how many fingers she has. How is that wrong? How can that ruin the shop's reputation?"

The girl starts sniffling again, and while she seems to be crying because she feels she's being treated unfairly by her superiors, it appears to be tinged with shock and fear that her very first client had only one hand. The owner wants to believe that her tears are out of sympathy toward the old lady who will likely never return, and she should have said something about how the girl should check when she holds the customer's hands by putting them out in front of her first. But if this bratty girl's only positive trait is an ability to empathize with someone else's misfortune, it might be worth keeping her on and coaching her, so she forces a smile.

"No, you did well."

The elderly woman walks along, her bag hanging on the crook of her arm, and absently stretches that arm out into the air. She looks at her thin, dry hand and admires the five fingernails glinting at the end. Each long fingernail is painted in navy, like the night sky or the chiffon blouse she's wearing, and each nail has its own unique color, pattern and amorphous design in yellow, light orange, white and light green, each starting at different coordinates and spreading out in concentric circles, and though the intention must have been to evoke fireworks in the night sky, viewed another way they appear to be many different kinds of fruit.

It's quite uncomfortable—it's the first time she's done something like this, especially the glued-on acrylic nails. It feels like someone else's flesh and bone have been grafted onto her hand. But the discomfort dies down when she looks at the pretty designs.

"It'll last at least two weeks, and you can shower and bathe as you normally would," the girl explained. "You can come back if it starts chipping or if you want to take them off, or I can give you some nail remover if you'd like to do it at home."

She allowed the young girl to take a picture of her hand. Watching the girl looking blissfully at her first masterpiece, she'd found herself cracking a smile, envious of the rude girl who had a pure and joyful side to her and who behaved however she wanted and wore her emotions on her sleeve.

She isn't going to show her nails to anyone. Not that she has anyone to show them to. Who knows, though? Maybe someone will see these nails as she taps her senior's pass on the bus or in the subway station, as she pays for a pack of gum at the convenience store, in these small moments of ordinary life. Maybe someone will spot the nails, then look up at her face, eyes widening in surprise. Maybe they will stay silent or clear their throat awkwardly, unable to verbalize their bias that it's not an appropriate look for someone her age. But right now, she likes these works of art placed on her broken, bruised, warped nails. Even more so because they're not real and will shine brightly, briefly, before disappearing.

Disappearing.

Maybe all living beings get to experience a bright shining moment at least once in their lives, precisely because they all crumble like overripe fruit, disappear like fireworks in the night sky.

And now is the time to live through all the losses she's been dealt.

So Ryu, it might not be my time to join you yet.

★ ★ ★ ★ ★

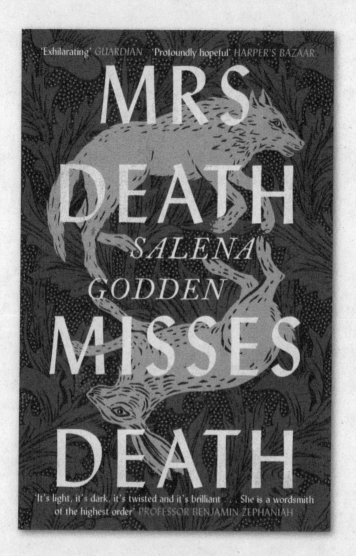

MRS
DEATH

SALENA
GODDEN

MISSES

DEATH

'Elegant'
Guardian

CANON‖GATE

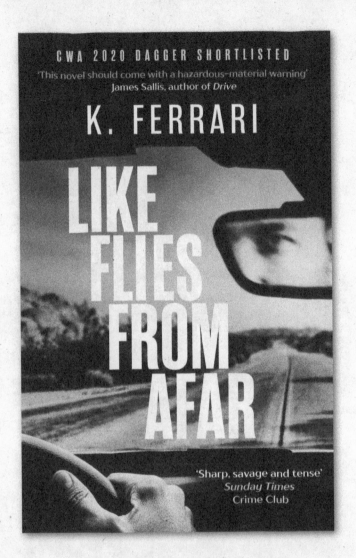

CWA 2020 DAGGER SHORTLISTED

'This novel should come with a hazardous-material warning'
James Sallis, author of *Drive*

K. FERRARI

LIKE FLIES FROM AFAR

'Sharp, savage and tense'
Sunday Times
Crime Club

'Existential and electric'
Los Angeles Times

CANON**GATE